I LIVE WITH YOU

CAROL EMSHWILLER

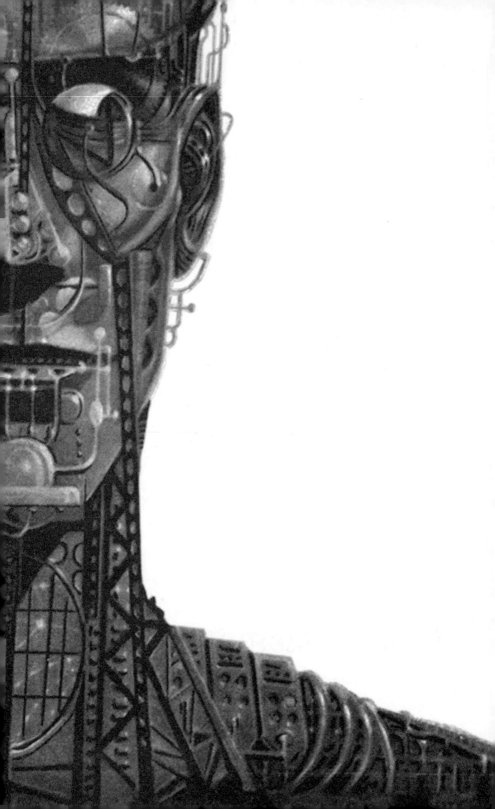

I LIVE WITH YOU

Carol Emshwiller

Tachyon Publications · San Francisco

I LIVE WITH YOU

INTRODUCTION © 2005 BY EILEEN GUNN

COVER ILLUSTRATION BY ED EMSHWILLER

COVER DESIGN BY ANN MONN
WITH THANKS TO CONNOR COCHRAN & JOHN BERRY

BOOK DESIGN BY ANN MONN

TACHYON PUBLICATIONS
1459 18TH STREET #139
SAN FRANCISCO, CA 94107
(415) 285-5615
www.tachyonpublications.com

EDITED BY JACOB WEISMAN

ISBN: 1-892391-25-2

PRINTED IN THE UNITED STATES OF AMERICA
BY PHOENIX COLOR CORPORATION

FIRST EDITION: 2005

0   9   8   7   6   5   4   3   2   1

To Ada, Amira, Barbara, Florence, Irene, Margaret, Maria, Marion, and Patsy.

WITH SPECIAL THANKS to Pat Murphy and Eileen Gunn, who braved dust and dirt and mold and mice and LOTS of spiders while looking through Ed Emsh's art for the sake of the cover of this book, and to Avon Swofford, who kept our spirits up even higher than they already were.

DO NOT REMOVE THIS TAG

Eileen Gunn

CAROL EMSHWILLER STORIES should come with warning labels: Do not operate heavy machinery while reading these stories. Avoid psychedelics when reading an Emshwiller story. Do not stay up all night, reading story after story by flashlight, under the covers. Because you could find yourself with an inexplicable desire to drive your heavy machine off-road into the mountains, flashing all your turn signals, defying gravity, and violating the social contract. You could permanently alter your brain chemistry, so that you are incapable of ignoring your perfectly reasonable impulse to move into a stranger's house and break him or her to your will. Deprived of sleep, myopic, and running on two D batteries, you could become convinced that subverting the natural order is not only an option, but a mandate.

Have Carol's stories always been this subversive? If asked, she says no, but why should we believe her? All those unreliable narrators—how can we trust this woman? I did a spot-check on a few stories. Well, maybe more than a few: they're pretty much irresistible, and a spot-check quickly turns into a couple of lost hours, sometimes days.

Her earliest work, a dozen stories published in the fifties and early sixties, remains uncollected, but the stories from the mid-sixties and early seventies, collected in *Joy in Our Cause* (1974), would subvert a Stepford wife. *Verging on the Pertinent* (1989) and *The Start of the End of It All* (1991), also collections, were obviously written by the same person as the first: someone who is funny, audacious, superbly imaginative, and in complete control of her material. Many of them document bizarre skirmishes in the battle of the sexes, no quarter given and none taken. The same could be said of her first novel, *Carmen Dog* (1990), in which the hapless but determined Pooch, evolving from dog to woman, seizes control from her master but still sleeps on the doormat.

After 1990, Carol's stories took an evolutionary turn, one of those sudden, life-related leaps that sometimes punctuate the work of an artist. Her husband, the artist and filmmaker Ed Emshwiller, died that year. Carol says, "My whole reason for writing changed for a while after my husband died. I needed people to live with. . . . As I began writing my western *Ledoyt* I didn't feel lonely at all. I was living with my characters more intimately than I ever had before in my whole writing life."

Ledoyt was published in 1995, and its sequel, *Leaping Man Hill*, in 1999. The ironic distance between Carol and her characters, evident in her previous stories, has been compressed. The tone of these novels is congruent with the earlier stories—Carol's unique writing voice is still there—but the reader finds herself participating more, feeling the character's emotions rather than observing them. *Report to the Men's Club and Other Stories*, though published in 2002, is not so much a document of Carol's continued evolution as a window on the process: it includes previously uncollected stories from the seventies and eighties, as well as work from the nineties and after. All of it wonderful and startling, all of it worth reading and rereading, as the month it has taken me to write this thousand words attests. In her novel *The Mount* (2002), she integrates this close-in characterization with a science-fiction plot, creating for the reader a disorientingly intimate journey into a bizarre relationship.

Carol Emshwiller has been producing brilliant stories for more than half a century, and she is more prolific now than ever: all of the stories in this book were written in the past several years. They are different from her earlier stories: more intent, less playful; sparer, more essential. Without sacrificing subtlety, they are more direct. Although Carol has not completely left behind the battle of the sexes, these new stories detail defections and private truces in a larger war: men and women engaged in hand-to-hand combat with life itself.

I sometimes visit Carol at her summer home in the Owens Valley of California, and she shows me around that spectacular high-desert terrain, where the rain evaporates before it hits the ground. Not too far from where she lives is the Ancient Bristlecone Pine Forest, home to the earth's oldest living inhabitants, trees that have survived for thousands of years in a climate so inhospitable that they have no predators or competition, growing so slowly that they become their own impermeable armor. She admires these trees, she says, because they live in a land of little water and bitter cold, and they thrive on it—not unlike some of the characters in this collection. Both the men and the women in these stories are stubborn, crafty, and courageous. They are tenacious, and they do seem to thrive under adverse conditions. Sometimes they are delusional, but aren't we all, sometimes?

When I visit, Carol leads me places I would never have gone alone: up onto an obsidian dome, across a river on a fallen tree, and over the John Muir Trail in a hailstorm. She has taken me into the High Sierra in search of a pie shop, and has made me an object of interest to the Inyo County sheriff's office. I can't say that she will subvert you in exactly the same way, but she will take you somewhere that expands your expectations, confronts your fears, and amuses you no end.

Seattle
January 26, 2005

TABLE OF CONTENTS

THE LIBRARY

W E'RE HEADED AWAY FROM war, past it, around and
beyond the enemy lines. We're circling behind
where the battle rages. Mostly we've hiked at night and
hidden during the day. We no longer hear or even see the
lights of explosions. We're glad we were given this duty. It's
been a restful week. Kind of like a camping trip.

We each have a bomb and there are ten of us. We have
several fire starters. That should be more than enough.
What we do is for the good of all mankind.

Theirs is the largest library in the world, but it's not our
books. They're not even in our language.

Even if we knew the language they're in a kind of
writing we can't read. It's full of squares and Os and
curlicues. We've been told many of the books are about the
art of war and that the poetry is bawdy. There's pictures of
nudes and of lovers in all possible positions.

I'm not to let any of us look at the books. Nor am I to
let one single book survive. There can be no peace and no
morality as long as these books exist.

There are statues at each corner of the building.
Caryatids along the porches. They say that, in the center
of the library, there's a reading room—a garden—open to
the sky. It's full of flowers. Birds. Even trees.

They say we'll recognize the library. It's larger than any other buildings. Our side thinks that when it's destroyed, their side will lose all momentum.

By now we have come to the beach. We're from the south. We've never seen the sea. We walk with our feet in the shallow water so our tracks will be washed away. When we camp for the day, we don't sleep much even though the sound of the water is soothing. We're distracted by all these new things. We watch the waves. We keep tasting the water—we can't believe it's salty. Some of us want to fish. Some of us want to taste the things on the shore but I don't trust them not to be poison.

Around midnight we hear singing, but it has no triads, no fifths. An accompanying instrument thunks and buzzes. I tell my group, "There. Listen. You can see what kind of people these are by this racket."

My group laughs. They're nervous and this odd music doesn't reassure them.

The library is across from an artificial pool so as to show it off with its reflection.

This has all been explained to us, and yet when we come upon the reflecting pool and the sparkling whiteness of the library, its painted frieze, the golden roof . . . we're silent. We've never seen such a building. It's evening and the sun makes everything pinkish-orange.

Seagulls wheel over our heads as if they are the avant-gardes of the books, their shrieks as alien as the language of the enemy.

We don't move. We just watch. The sun goes down. Stars come out. Nobody says anything. The moon rises and reflects in the pool. We should move back and find a place to camp but we can't tear ourselves away. We sit where we are, fall asleep towards morning, then wake to watch the sunrise. I don't ask the group what they think about burning it down. I don't want to know. Besides, it doesn't matter what they think.

After the sunrise we load up our weapons and cross to the edge of the pool, march right into it, two by two, and splash across to the library. We don't care if they hear us or not.

Close up, the eyes of the caryatids stare at us, seem to warn us that the library is not for the likes of us. Each of them has one bare breast. I tell my men not to look.

We head to the main doors. They're of carved wood. Easy to burn down with our fire starters. (We don't look at them. Who knows what might be carved there.) We would have bashed through them, but they're open. We walk right in.

We're as awed by the inside as we were with the outside. We become aware of how dirty and smelly we are, how we're dripping on their mosaic floor. The sun, shining through the stained glass of the clerestory windows, leaves odd colors on the walls, tables—on the people. The librarians look up, but they stay calm. Behind them there are shelves and shelves of books. The books are dark and dusty, and look old, as do the librarians. And—we can't believe it's true—all the librarians have one bare breast, sometimes the right and sometimes the left. Now, in front of us men, they don't even try to hide themselves.

We point our guns, but I'm the only one that shoots. I shoot out one of the stained-glass windows. I surprise my own group even more than I surprise the librarians. My group all jump while the librarians just look though some hold their books closer like shields.

One librarian comes up to us, (bare-breasted, brazen as could be) holds her book, a large heavy one, but she doesn't try to cover herself with it. She looks like the enemy—they all have colorless hair and colorless eyes. She addresses us in what seems like two or three different languages, one after the other. Finally in ours. She whispers. She tells us to keep quiet. She points to a sign that says SILENCE even in our language. Then she says, "We have nothing to do with wars in here."

"You lie."

I whisper, too, though I didn't mean to.

She says, "This is a place of truths."

"Your books are full of lies. You, yourself, are a lie."

"Look around you. Does this look like lies?"

I look at the sun pouring down from the window I shot out. The real color of the sun comes in whereas the other windows show false colors. My shot is the only truth here. I point to the square of sunlight under the broken window. "There is the truth," I say.

Her face is narrow and fierce. She wears a robe down to her ankles. Surely it would tangle in bushes if she tries to walk where there are no paths. These people are, clearly, just as we've been told, overly civilized. A civilization at its final gasp. You can always tell by the clothes.

I imagine what the book she hugs so tightly must have in it. Secrets of sex, and perhaps of battles won.

We weren't told what to do with the librarians. I suppose it's up to my discretion.

She says, "There are all sorts of truths."

"You wouldn't know a truth if it was written in stone."

One of my group says, "If it were in stone, it would be true."

I don't answer such a platitude. I tell my group, to get out their fire starters. I say it for all to hear. If the librarians want to escape, it's up to them.

My group hesitates. They don't want to do their job. They take off their packs to get their fire starters, but more slowly than they should. Grandeur and beauty have confused them. They have lost sight of their principles. I'm tempted to shoot out another window to remind them which side they're on.

The librarians hold their books as though they're weapons. Some have thick covers and metal corners and look heavy.

I shoot again, but this time I don't know what I hit. That fierce librarian attacks me with her book before I can see if I hit out another window or not. Next thing I know my nose is pressed into a mosaic of a triton with an octopus hooked in it. I almost think I'm back at the seashore. Art lies. It always lies. These are—I see clearly—groups of small stones, white and black over blue waves. A shot at the floor would have scattered them back into their reality.

I get up on my knees and point my gun down at the false octopus, but one of my own men turns on me and hits me with the butt of his gun.

I come-to bound to a homemade chair. I'm in a simple room no better than our barracks. They say the librarians do live simply. They say the library is their only luxury. There are shelves along the walls as if for books, but with potted plants on them. Some of the pots would make good weapons.

I don't need my group. I can destroy the library by myself. And if I don't have bombs, I can make new ones. They didn't send out a munitions expert for nothing.

I begin to work on the knots that tie me to the chair. They've been tied by women. I easily loosen them. My jaw hurts where my comrade hit me. Have they all mutinied? Do I have a single friend? Is it because the library is too beautiful? But they told us it would be.

First thing I grab the largest pot to use as a weapon. I pick one with a strong looking plant and hold it by the woody stalk. Then I look out the window to see where I am.

And there's another lie—right on the wall of the hut next door. A painting of trees and flowers, a stream even. As if trying to make this desert place like my land down south, and not succeeding. They may have the library, but we have the forest and the mountains. The painting makes me homesick. But then I realize I'm falling into their trap: taking a painting as the truth. I don't let myself think of home.

I open the door as quietly as possible. There's another room. A writing room. Desk and paper, ink. . . . Also an easel with the start of a painting. It's the portrait of a child. One of their kind—almost white hair and light eyes. I hate that pale, insipid look. I splash the ink on it. I wish for more ink and then I see there's paint I can smear.

I feel good afterwards. I've struck a blow for truth. I pick up my plant-weapon and go in search of chemicals for a bomb, and maybe food, too.

I creep outside carefully, and there is the back of the library—as impressive as the front. If I had even a little of the gold of the roof I'd be a wealthy man. I think to climb a pillar, grab some golden tiles and go home. Bypass the war altogether. But then I think, after I bomb it the gold will be even easier to pick up.

I go into a different hut. Looking for a kitchen, or a shed with fertilizer. I find another writing room. There's no painting so I spill the ink all over the writing.

In the kitchen, I find a paste with what looks like scallions mixed in it. God knows what they eat or if this is for the cat. Or, for all I know, their pet rat. I eat it anyway.

Then I look for chemicals. But, of course, the labels on things are different. I have to try everything by smell—even by taste. I make a concoction, but I'm not sure about it. I hope it really is a bomb.

I grab my (maybe) bomb and my plant weapon and start out again when I hear the door open and there's a librarian, a young one.

How can such a pale creature look so beautiful?

Thank goodness her breast is covered—or she'd be in more trouble than she knows.

I can see on her face she has passed through the room where I damaged the writing. She's half my size, but she comes after me with her fists. I swing the plant. The pot flies off and dirt flies all over. She gets a face full. Dirt in her eyes and nose and mouth. Next thing, here I am, trying to clean her up. And saying I'm sorry—in my own language.

She can't answer in any. Her mouth is too full of dirt.

I find the water jar. I lean her over a basin. I use a clean cloth to get things out of her eyes. They're not colorless as we keep saying. They're tan with little greenish radiating lines. Actually they're almost exactly the same color as her hair. Her skin is tan also. She's all of a piece. You could say the same about me, black hair and black eyes, dark skin.

It takes a long time to clean her up. After, we sit on cushions across from each other, both of us exhausted. She's a mess. Her hair is wet and hanging down, her shirt front is sopping. I'm a mess, too.

Now she says, Thank you—in my language. And I say again, I'm sorry.

She looks to be as taken with me as I am with her. Both of us dazzled with the odd, the unknown—I with my shaved head and top knot and my damaged hands, and she with her almost white hair flying out around her shoulders and her hands soft as a baby's. She must do nothing but read and paint.

Both of us hardly dare to glance at each other—especially after being so close, eye to eye, my arms holding her. I have looked in her ears, in her nose, I've helped her rinse her mouth.

We sit silent. Finally she says, "I'll make tea. I'll get you something to eat."

(I don't care what it is, I'll eat it.)

"Are you going to tell them I'm here?"

"I don't know."

"I would have hit you with the heavy pot if it hadn't fallen off."

"Yes, but you helped me after."

"I don't know books. I prefer reality."

"I only know books."

"Do you want to see the rest of the world? I'll take you. Help me destroy the library and I'll take you with me."

"Why? Why destroy it?"

"It's all lies. Your life is a lie. I'll bet you do nothing but sit all the time. Did you ever play?"

"Of course I did."

"What did you play?"

"We drew and painted. Sewed. Cooked. Made things. I had a doll."

"That's not play. Play is top-o-the-roost, knick-knack, capture flags . . . I don't think you had any fun at all."

"But I did."

"You don't even know you weren't happy."

"But I was."

I feel sorry for all the librarians.

"Come with me. I'll show you happiness. I'll teach you to play. And you know bombing the library will be useful to everybody. The pieces of marble can go to make many smaller houses. The roof can make everybody rich. The painted birds and butterflies pressed into the walls. . . . There must be a hundred. A hundred people could each have one. You could have one yourself. You could wear it in your hair."

I see I've given her something to think about.

"Give the little people marble and gold. Spread the beauty around so there's some for everybody—and keep some for yourself."

Every time she looks at me I can see her fascination in her eyes. I wonder if she's ever seen a shaved head and topknot before. She keeps looking at my hands. I always did like my hands. I'm proud of my scars. All have been achieved honorably.

I'm everything the opposite of her. She's even small for one of the enemy, while I'm tall for one of us.

She says, "We thought your eyes were so dark they were blind to all things delicate and light. We said you were too tall to be strong, but you're as if made of ropes."

"We thought you were blind for the opposite reason." Then I say, "My group . . . they betrayed me. Where are they? What did you do with them?"

(No doubt by now all my men want are books and bare breasted librarians.)

"We fed them periwinkles and clams. They spit them out and ate their own dried up things. We walked them back to the beach where there are cottages. Most of us went with them. We thought you were safely tied up."

"How many librarians stayed?"

"Six. And me."

The perfect time to bomb it and set fires.

I talk to her about chemicals. She helps me read the labels. I find things to use as fire starters. I even find stuff for a few bombs.

We work well side by side. I think what it would be like bringing her back to my people. How shocked my people would be.

"What we'll do is put these little sacks all around, inside and outside the library. It's time. It's already getting dark. Let's do it now."

She says, "There's nobody there at night."

"Good. First you can pick your favorite book to keep just for yourself."

I feel good that I can give her something. I'm going to make sure she gets a butterfly or a bird, and some of the gold.

She says, "We'll need a lamp. There aren't any windows except those high stained-glass ones. Books take up all the wall space."

We gather up the little packages and tubes and carry them to the library. Right away I climb up and put some under the roof. She's never seen anything like my climbing. All I need is a little finger grip and toe grip. My own men can't do that. I see I impress her even more than before.

When I place the last package and climb down, I can't resist the admiration in her eyes, I lean to kiss her. She looks as if she's leaning to kiss me, but she turns away at the last minute.

We light our lamp and go inside. Right away she takes out a huge book.

"We can't bring *that!*"

"I just want to show you some pictures. There are lots like this here, but this book is the best."

The book is so big she has to put it on a special stand. She opens it and there they are—in gold leaf, or looks like it, a golden woman and a golden man. Naked. The woman is handing the man grapes or dates, and he reaches, not for them, but towards her breast. It's as lewd as we always said their drawings are. But the green of the trees is as beautiful as the gold, so is the blue of the sky, as though green and blue could be as valuable as gold. The landscape is more like my world than like hers. It's a picture you could fall right into—and would want to except for the naked couple. If I were there I'd hurry away behind the trees in the foreground.

She turns the page and the next is even worse than the first. It's as if you're standing on a higher hill than before, in the shadow of pine trees, looking down. This time the couple is farther away, but you can see the golden man has his hand on the woman's golden breast now, and the grapes or dates are on the ground, forgotten.

Why is she showing me this? And she looks so young and innocent? She isn't. Art has ruined her. She knows everything already. Probably more than I do. No wonder they want me to destroy the library.

I don't want her to turn to the next page. Nor the next and the next. I can imagine what they'll be. And why look when we can do?

I grab her and throw her down . . . on the make-believe octopus. I drop on top of her. Kiss her—hard.

At first she's too shocked to react. She doesn't seem to know what's happening, but then she struggles. She bites my lip. I pull back and she yells, first a wordless shout and then, "No! Help!" If she keeps on making a racket, whatever other librarians are left here will come. I cover her mouth with my hand. She bites my hand this time and knees me. I'm the one should be yelling No.

"I'll let you go if you don't shout."

"You're an animal."

"It's you, are an animal. How could you show me those pictures? And why? If not for. . . ." But we don't have words for that—not ones you can say to women.

"I wanted you to see something beautiful. I thought if you saw them you might not want to burn them."

"I want to burn them all the more. Are all the books like this? Full of nakedness and corruption?"

"Let me read something to you. Let me find the book—
the one I'd choose if I could have one of my own."

She goes straight to a small, hand-sized book. She
holds it close to the lamp and begins to read, translating
as she goes. Even in my own language I don't understand
it at all.

> *Last to leave and first to come.*
> *A guessing game of death or life.*
> *Leaves of summer, leaves of spring.*
> *We fall but in our own ways.*
> *Neither like streams nor leaves.*

Perhaps the meaning is lost in translation. I say, "Poetry
lies as much as pictures do."

"We think it's more true than truth."

"There can't be such a thing?"

Even so . . . even after the bad pictures and the
meaningless poetry . . . even so I still like her. And she . . .
even after I threw her down and almost raped her. She still
likes me. I can see it on her face.

I say, "I like you. In spite of the pictures. But I don't
suppose you can like me."

"I don't know what to think."

"I don't either but I like you anyway. But I don't even
know your name."

"Yawn," she says.

"What!"

"My name is Yawn."

That's an ugly word in our language. I can hardly make
myself say it. I wonder what my name means in hers.

"I'm Gabb."

"Bless water."

Should I have said the same after she said her name?
Why bless? And by what crippled god?

"Let me read you this other poem."

Joy is in the view from above
As houses seen by eagles
As after storms or in them,
Seen as if you are the whirlwind.
Be such.

It doesn't make sense to me anymore than the other one did. I'll destroy this gobbledygook. "Let's get on with the burning. We'll start with that big book."

I should have known better than to start with that book. Even the little book of poems can be a weapon. And I'm not ready for it. She hits me hard in the stomach. I lean in pain, but then my training kicks in. I hit her so hard she flies across the mosaic floor into the shelves of books beyond.

I go to her. I call, "Yawn. Yawn." I don't bother keeping quiet anymore.

Before I pick her up, I take out the fire starters. I throw out several in different directions. Then I carry her out to the pool. Halfway across it I put her on the edge of it and turn to watch the fire. It starts fast and when it reaches the bombs I set around the edges and under the roof, the blasts begin. Not as large as I'd have wished them to be.

Of course the librarians come, but six women are no match for someone like me. One problem, though, I have to keep my eyes shut because of all those bare breasts. I'm afraid I might touch one.

They trip me. I fall into the pool. They're water people and I'm not. I'm helpless in it. They hold my head under. It's Yawn yells for them to stop just when I'm choking. They pull me to the edge and Yawn turns me over and pumps the water out. It takes a while before I can breathe.

The little homemade bombs are still going off now and then as the fire reaches them, but they're much too small. The building won't come down. Some of the librarians stand near the carved doors, their silhouettes outlined against the flames inside. They don't dare go in yet.

Nobody's paying attention to me. I roll over on my

back and watch the dawn come, turning everything pinkish again. But the library is a mess, black from smoke, some corners are broken, but my bombs were too feeble to bring down the walls.

It's still an imposing sight in an entirely different way. The caryatids still look down in disapproval from over their bare breasts. A few gold tiles have fallen from the roof but nobody is rushing to pick them up even though just one would make a person rich. The librarians walk right past them.

Yawn sits beside me. I tell her I didn't mean to hit her so hard. She says, "I know."

Finally the fires settle down enough for the librarians to wrap wet scarves around their faces and go in. Yawn stays with me. Says, "I don't understand why you wanted to destroy it."

"To show your side we can bring down your most magnificent building."

"But you didn't. We don't even have any soldiers to protect it, and you didn't. Even so you failed."

"But look what one single man. . . . I, alone. . . ."

"You failed."

"I'll bring you a bird. I'll bring you gold."

"What would you do if you were a golden man and lived in those pictures?"

"And you were the golden woman."

"Would you throw me down like you did?"

I'm thinking I would put my hand on her breast, but I don't say it. "Never again."

"Or maybe you'd melt me down and have me made into coins. Or you'd melt yourself down."

"I don't think unreal things. Besides, I'd rather be of use after I die. My skin gone for leather. My bones for spoons. I'd never become anything for beauty. Promise you won't let that happen to me."

"We're not going to kill you. I won't let us."

"Let's escape together."

She's tempted. "What would you do, go steal tiles?"

"I'd rather have you than golden tiles."

That pleases her. She will come. She says, "Hurry," takes my hand to pull me into the bushes by the side of the pool, but I pull her in the other direction. I want to see what the librarians are doing in there. Maybe I can keep them from putting out fires.

She tries to hold me back. "But you said. . . ."

"Your art tells lies and I lie, too."

Inside, the library is full of smoke. Librarians are stamping out fires, putting rugs and wet towels over books. Some bring smoldering books out and dump them in the pool. Some books are so large it takes two or even three librarians to carry them.

Those still inside have wet scarves around their faces but Yawn and I don't. We begin to cough right away. A librarian hits me from behind and knocks me into a still burning book. Two and Yawn drag me out and dump me in the pool to stop my burning clothes, my burning topknot.

They argue about me. Mostly in their own language. Then one says, on purpose in my language, "He's not worth the trouble. Finally they say to Yawn—in my language, "He's yours to do with as you wish." They sound disgusted.

They get thongs to tie my ankles—loose enough so I can walk a little. The fires are out in the library and Yawn hurries me through the smoke to the central garden. It's untouched except a little smoky. She doesn't say a word. She ties me to a bench and leaves.

There are trees in there. Flowering bushes. A birdbath but no birds. Still too smoky. I watch the little fountain. I don't try to get loose. I'm tied so I can lie down. I do.

Finally Yawn comes back with a lumpy awkward bundle and with tea and food. She gives me the tea and a fishy smelling sort of cake and dates. I don't feel like eating, especially not a fishy cake, but the tea is good.

Then she starts unpacking the things she brought, a folding stool, a folding easel, a wooden slab, long as her arm, to paint on. An odd thing to be doing after what's been happening. I'm an exotic creature fit for a zoo. She can't wait to get me down on a flat surface. To put on some wall, I suppose. Which makes me wonder what she'll do with the real me after. Will the painting take my place?

She begins, even as I'm sipping tea.

She works in spurts and then looks at me and thinks. Finally she shows me what she's done so far. There I am, just begun, but even so you can see it's me. You can see my topknot curling down behind my ear and then over my shoulder though now it's burned off. She has my eyes almost finished. They're like holes in the board. I suppose all of it will look like a hole through the board when she's done.

She starts to paint again. We're quiet and then she says, "I want you to be. . . . I wish you could be. . . ."

"I'll never be."

Whatever it was she was going to say, she'd hate me if I was. She loves me because I'm not like her. Same reason I like her.

Then, again, she turns the painting towards me. She sits beside me to study it. Now my face is almost finished.

She keeps looking over at me as though wondering what I think about it. I'm impressed. Not only with how much it looks like me but that it only took her a short time to paint it. I'm thinking I might steal it if I have the chance.

But I'm angry with myself for thinking it. I say, "This is a lie. Does a flower need a painting of itself?" I hear myself saying, "Do I need this?" even as I'm thinking that I do.

At that thought I bang my fists against the edge of the bench.

"You hate my painting."

"I like it. I like it. I shouldn't, but I do. But where I come from images are not allowed."

"How can that be?"

"And no bare breasts."

"Are breasts bad?"

"You'll learn that if you come home with me."

She says again, "Bless water."

"We don't bless things like water."

"Your language has no word for what we mean by blessing. And no word for asking somebody to come see a sight. No word for a sky full of birds and we all look up. Even my name, you can't guess its many meanings."

"Tell me."

But she says, "You keep saying we should love the real, but the real disappears. One of these days this painting will be all that's left of you."

Is that a warning?

Then we hear a great rushing sound, loud as thunder right overhead, and the ground shakes and the painting falls and the stoa surrounding the garden . . . every pillar breaks.

Then it comes again. Worse.

After that, silence. Not even the cry of a seagull.

We wait, looking at each other.

And it comes again, just as we thought it would.

We are safe in the center of devastation. Everything is already flattened around us, but we don't move.

So it isn't me that makes the golden tiles for all to pick up, that buries the books in debris—though I would have wished it were me.

It won't be easy to leave the garden considering what's piled up around us.

I say, "I need to be free now. I can't be tied up."

She can't answer. She can't move.

"I can't go anywhere. Look around you. We're both prisoners."

Odd how the garden itself is untouched. The birdbath and sundial still stand. The trees. There's even water still spouting in the fountain though not as much.

And here's another aftershock.

"Let me go. What harm can I do now? We can't even get out of here. Not easily."

The library looks like piles of talus from back in my home mountains. Unstable to try to climb over. I can but she can't without my help.

Finally she unties me. She's so shaky she can hardly do it. I make her drink the rest of my tea. For a few minutes she can only talk her own language. I say a few words in mine to remind her. I say, "Don't worry, only this large stone building is destroyed. The librarians are most likely safe and I'll wager your little house still stands."

I take off my shirt, take it to the fountain, rinse it a bit first, and then wet it and wipe her face.

After a while I leave her sitting there and go to examine how hemmed in we are. I leave the dates and cakes beside her. I tell her to eat them if she wants to.

All the arcade is collapsed. I feel as if I'm in my own private grove. This is my fountain. My grape arbor, still climbing up its frame. (The frame stands and yet the wall is rubble.) I make the complete circuit. I see a nest with baby birds in it. I wonder if the parents will come back. Whiffs of smoke and dust still rise now and then. But getting out of here doesn't look good. I can do it, but Yawn can't without my help. Now she's my prisoner.

I pick a bunch of grapes to bring to her in case she wants something cool and sweet.

It's already getting too dark for climbing the rubble—or for painting. I wonder if she'll ever finish my portrait.

I think to build a fire but the garden is so immaculate there are no dead branches and no dead leaves. Trust these overly refined people to have everything all cleaned up.

I come back, sit beside her and give her the grapes. I put my arm around her and she doesn't flinch away. I say, "It won't be easy getting out."

I feel like First Man and she First Woman. They have just crawled out of the earth after the fires and floods of formation, all around them devastation, and it's up to them to clean up and populate the world. Up to Yawn and me. I hold her. I don't say anything. There's the sunset. We can't see the sun setting behind the rubble, but we see the pink and purple sky. She glows pinkish gold. I say, "That book . . . and us. . . ."

She says, "That book is burned. They said it was the first to go."

"That was them wasn't it?"

She says, "I was named for her."

I say, "I was named for a god of war." Then I say it, "This is our garden. We'll live here."

She leans her head against my shoulder. "How will we eat?"

"The fig tree, the grapes. . . . I'll build a shelter out of rubble and tree branches. I'll make us a bed of young boughs."

Then I, like the golden man, forget the grapes and dates and put my hand on her breast.

"And will you like the things I like?"

"If I must."

That night we love each other.

Towards morning we hear cries from beyond the rubble. We hear both her language and mine. My group is there, calling out to me.

I keep silent, but Yawn yells back that we're here and all right.

"We're coming for you as soon as it's daylight."

Yawn turns to me. "That doesn't change anything."

"Out there I'll be a prisoner."

I'm wondering: First Man and First Woman? How did they end up? I'm glad that book is burned. I wouldn't want to see pages three and four and five and especially not ten, eleven, thirteen. . . . And yet I do wonder how it ended.

At dawn we hear them pulling at the rubble. We hear shouts and curses from my men. We hear women singing. Trust these people to be singing no matter what. I wouldn't be surprised if they were dancing, too, maybe even dancing as they remove stones.

Yawn says, "Come, we'll help. It's by the arbor that they're working," but the longer it takes the happier I'll be.

"Escape with me. We'll climb the opposite side. Here with your people, I don't know how to be."

"I'll teach you. And the books will tell you."

"The books are gone."

"Then we'll write some more."

Is anything ever really destroyed, human beings being what they are?

She says, "Come help." She's scrabbling at the stones as if our lives depended on being rescued.

I say, "You want to leave our garden."

But I help. It's inevitable. We *will* be rescued.

We move stones in silence, then take a rest. Drink and wash and eat figs. I say, "I wish you were finishing the painting instead."

"So you *do* like it."

"I like what you're doing."

After a few minutes rest, Yawn begins to work at the rubble again.

I could cross by myself. Faster than Yawn and faster than those trying to get to us.

I head for the fountain and take a big drink. I put figs in my pockets. I leap on the rocks on the opposite side from where they're coming for us. It's the worst side, higher than the other. I can leap from rock to rock in a way most people can't. I'm used to mountains and unstable talus.

Here and there I see gold tiles. One. Just one—for my mother.

But Yawn has seen me. I hear her give a dreadful cry. It lasts a long wailing time. It stuns me. It stops me that Yawn could cry such a cry. It can't be Yawn.

I'm teetering on the remains of a pillar. I never fall. I've never fallen.

I open my eyes to a sky bluer than blue, to grass greener than green, to a landscape like home only more so. I hear the silvery sound of a stream. I see its glitter. I look down

19

at myself and see I'm naked and I'm gold. I couldn't even guess how valuable I am.

At first I try to hide my nakedness—as though someone watched, as I did, from behind the trees. But then I see, in the distance, a woman coming out from beyond the cedars. She wears a white flowing garment and has one breast bare.

My figs are on the ground in front of me but I'm not hungry.

Last night we already did as if turning the pages of this book. Now we'll do it again. Perhaps there are more pages than I guessed at when I first saw it. Perhaps I'll find out how it ends.

I LIVE WITH YOU AND YOU DON'T KNOW IT

I LIVE IN YOUR HOUSE and you don't know it. I nibble at your food. You wonder where it went . . . where your pencils and pens go. . . . What happened to your best blouse. (You're just my size. That's why I'm here.) How did your keys get way over on the bedside table instead of by the front door where you always put them? You *do* always put them there. You're careful.

I leave dirty dishes in the sink. I nap in your bed when you're at work and leave it rumpled. You thought you had made it first thing in the morning and you had.

I saw you first when I was hiding out at the bookstore. By then I was tired of living where there wasn't any food except the muffins in the coffee bar. In some ways it was a good place to be . . . the reading, the music. I never stole. Where would I have taken what I liked? I didn't even steal back when I lived in a department store. I left there forever in my same old clothes though I'd often worn their things at night. When I left, I could see on their faces that they were glad to see such a raggedy person leave. I could see they wondered how I'd gotten in in the first place. To tell the truth, only one person noticed me. I'm hardly ever noticed.

But then, at the bookstore, I saw you: Just my size, Just my look. And you're as invisible as I am. I could see that nobody noticed you just as hardly anybody notices me.

I followed you home—a nice house just outside of town. If I wore your clothes, I could go in and out and everybody would think I was you. But I wondered, how get in in the first place? I thought it would have to be in the middle of the night and I'd have to climb in a window.

But I don't need a window. I hunch down and walk in right behind you. You'd think somebody that nobody ever notices would notice other people, but you don't.

Once I'm in, right away I duck into the hall closet.

You have a cat. Isn't that just like you? And just like me also. I would have had one were I you.

The first few days are wonderful. Your clothes are to my taste. Your cat likes me (right away better than he likes you). Right away I find a nice place in your attic. Not an attic, more a crawl space but I'm used to hunching over. In fact that's how I walk around almost all the time. The space is narrow and long, but it has little windows at each end. Out one, I can look right into a treetop. I think an apple tree. If it was the right season I could reach out and pick an apple. I brought up your quilt. I saw you looking puzzled after I took the hall rug. I laughed to myself when you changed the locks on your doors. Right after that I took a photo from the mantel. Your mother I presume. I wanted you to notice it was gone, but you didn't.

I bring up a footstool. I bring up cushions, one by one until I have four. I bring up magazines, straight from the mail box, before you have a chance to read them.

What I do all day? Anything I want to. I dance and sing and play the radio and TV.

When you're home, I come down in the evening, stand in the hall and watch you watch TV.

I wash my hair with your shampoo. Once, when you came home early, I almost got caught in the shower. I hid in the hall closet, huddled in with the sheets, and watched you find the wet towel—the spilled shampoo.

You get upset. You think: I've heard odd thumps for weeks. You think you're in danger, though you try hard to talk yourself out of it. You tell yourself it's the cat, but you know it's not.

You get a lock for your bedroom door—a dead bolt. You have to be inside to push it closed.

I have left a book open on the couch, the print of my head on the couch cushion. I've pulled out a few gray hairs to leave there. (We're both graying, though you less than I.) I have left a half full wine glass on the counter. I have left your underwear (which I wore) on the bathroom floor, dirty socks under the bed, a bra hanging on the towel rack. I left a half-eaten pizza on the kitchen counter. (I ordered out and paid with your stash of quarters, though I know where you keep your secret twenties.)

I set all your clocks back fifteen minutes but I set your alarm clock to four in the morning. I hid your reading glasses. I pull buttons off your sweaters and put them where your quarters used to be. Your quarters I put in your button box.

Normally I try not to bump and thump in the night but I'm tired of your little life. At the bookstore and grocery store at least things happened all day long. You keep watching the same TV programs. You go off to work. You make enough money, (I see the bank statements) but what do you do with it? I want to change your life into something worth watching.

I do begin to thump, bump, and groan and moan. (I've been feeling like groaning and moaning for a long time, anyway.) Maybe I'll bring you a man.

I'll buy you new clothes and take away the old ones, so you'll *have* to wear the new ones. The new clothes will be red and orange and with stripes and polka dots. When I get through with you, you'll be real . . . or at least realer.

People will notice you. Your red cheeks. Your frown.

Now you groan and sigh as much as I do. You think: This can't be happening. I've lived here and all these years nothing has happened.

You think: What about the funny sounds coming from the crawl space? You think: I don't dare go up there by myself, but who could I get to go with me? (You don't have any friends that I know of. You're like me in that.)

Monday you go off to work wearing a fuzzy blue top and red leather pants. You had a hard time finding a combination without stripes or big flowers or dots on it.

I watch you from your kitchen window. I'm heating up your leftover coffee. I'm making toast. I use up all the butter. You thought there was plenty for the next few days.

You almost caught me the time I came home late with packages. I had to hide behind the curtains. I could tell that my feet showed out the bottom, but you didn't notice.

Another time you saw me duck into the closet but you didn't dare open the door. You hurried upstairs to your bedroom and pushed the deadbolt. That evening you didn't come down at all. You skipped supper. I watched TV . . . any show I wanted.

I can go in your bedroom and lock you out just like you locked me out. I could bring up a good supper and the cat. Then you'd have to go sleep in the crawl space. It's not bad up there. Lots of your things are handy, a bedside lamp, a clock. . . .

I put another deadbolt on the outside of your bedroom door. Just in case. It's way up high. I don't think you'll notice. It might come in handy.

(Lacy underwear with holes in lewd places. Nudist magazines. Snails and sardines—smoked oysters. Neither one of us like them. All the things I get with your money are for you. I don't steal.)

How get through Christmas all by yourself? You're lonely enough for both of us. You wrap empty boxes in Christmas paper just to be festive. You buy a tree, a small one. It's artificial and comes with lights that glimmer on and off. The cat and I come down to sleep near its glow.

But the man. The one I want to bring to you. I look over the personals. I write letters to possibilities but, as I'm taking them to the post office, I see somebody. He limps and wobbles. (The way he lurches sideways looks like sciatica to me. Or maybe arthritis.) He needs a haircut and a shave. He's wearing an old plaid jacket and he's all knees and elbows. There's a countrified look about him. Nobody wears plaid around here.

I limp behind him. Watch him go into one of those little apartments behind a main house and over a garage. It's not far from our house.

It can't be more than one room. I could never creep around in that place and not be noticed.

A country cousin. Country uncle more likely, he's older than we are. Is he capable of what I want him for?

Next day I watch him in the grocery store. Like us, he buys living-alone kind of food, two apples, a tomato, crackers, oatmeal. Poor people's kind of food. I get in line with him at the checkout. I bump into him on purpose as he pays and peek into his wallet. That's all he has—just enough for what he buys. He counts out the change a penny at a time and he hardly has a nickel left over. I get ready to give him a bit extra if he needs it.

He's such an ugly, rickety man. . . . Perfect.

There's no reason to go into his over–the-garage room, but I want to. This is important. I need to see who he is.

I use our credit card to open his lock.

What a mess. He needs somebody like us to look after him. His bed is piled with blankets. The room isn't very well heated. The bathroom has a curtain instead of a door. There's no tub or even shower. I check the hot water in the sink. It says HOT, but both sides come out cold. All he has is a hot plate. No refrigerator. There's two windows, but no curtains. Isn't that just like a man. I could climb up on the back fence and see right in.

There's nothing of the holidays here. Nothing of any holidays and not a single picture of a relative. And, like our house, nothing of friends. You and he are made for each other.

What to do to show I've been here? But I don't feel much like playing tricks. And it's so messy he wouldn't notice, anyway.

It's cold. I haven't taken my coat off all through this. I make myself a cup of tea. (There's no lemons and no milk. Of course.) I sit in his one chair. It's painted ugly green. All his furniture is as if picked up on the curb and his bedside table is one of those fruit boxes. As I sit and sip, I check his magazines. They look as though stolen out of somebody's garbage. I'm shivering. No wonder he's out. (I suppose it's not easy to shave. He'd have to heat the water on the hot plate.)

He needs a cat. Something to sleep on his chest to keep him warm like your cat does with me. Should I bring ours over? It would take you a week to notice he was gone. I could nibble at the cat food. I have already.

I have our groceries in my backpack. I leave two oranges and a doughnut in plain sight beside the hot plate. I leave several of our quarters.

I leave a note: I put in our address but not our telephone number. (He doesn't have a phone anyway.) I sign your name. I write: Come for Christmas. Two o'clock. I'll be wearing red leather pants! Your neighbor, Nora.

(I wonder which of us should wear those pants.)

I clean up a little bit but not so much that he'd notice if he's not a noticing person. Besides, people only notice when things are dirty. They never notice when things are cleaner.

As I walk home, I see you on your way out. We pass each other. You look right at me. I'm wearing your green sweater and your black slacks. We look at each other, my brown eyes to your brown eyes. Only difference is, your hair is pushed back and mine hangs down over my forehead and I have to admit my nose is less aristocratic. You go right on by. I turn and look back. You don't. I laugh behind my hand that you had to wear those red leather pants and a black and white striped top.

He's too timid and too self-deprecating to come. He doesn't like to limp in front of people and he's ashamed not to have enough money hardly even for his food, and not to have a chance to shave and take a bath. Though if he's scared by me coming into his room, he might come. He might want to see who Nora is and if the address is real. His pretext will be that he wants to thank you for the food and quarters. He might even want to give them back. He might be one of those rich people who live as if they were poor. I should have looked for money or bank books. I will next time.

When the doorbell rings who else could it be?
    You open the door.
    "Are you Nora?"
    "Yes?"
    "I want to thank you."
    I knew it. I suppose he wants more money.
    "But I want to bring your quarters back. That was kind of you but I don't need them."
    You don't know what to say. You suspect it's all because of me. That I've, yet again, made your life difficult. You wonder what to do. He doesn't look dangerous but you never can tell. You want to get even with me some way. You suppose, if he *is* dangerous, it'll be bad for both of us so you ask him in.
    He hobbles into your living room. You say, sit down, that you'll get tea. You're stalling for time.
    He still holds the handful of quarters. He puts them on the coffee table. It's hard for him to sit. Good the chair

has arms.

You don't know how those quarters got to him or even if they really are your quarters. "No, no," you say, and "Where did these come from?"

"They were in my room with a note from you and this address. You said, Come for Christmas."

You wonder what I'll like least. Do I want you to invite him to stay for supper. Unlikely, though, since you only have one TV dinner and you know I know that.

"Somebody is playing a joke on me. But the tea. . . ."

You need help getting started so I trip you in the hall as you come back into the room. Everything goes down. Too bad, too, because you'd used your good china in spite of how this man looks.

Of course he pushes himself up and hobbles to you and helps pick up the things and you. You say you could make more but he says, It doesn't matter. Then you both go out to the kitchen. I go, too. Sidling. Slithering. The cat slides in with us. Both yours and his glasses are thick. I'm counting on your blindness. I squat down. He puts the broken cups on a corner of the counter. You get out two more. He says, these are too nice. You say they're Mother's. He says, "You shouldn't use the Rosenthal, not for me."

There now, are you both rich yet never use your money?

The cat jumps on the table and you swipe him off. No wonder he likes me better then you. I always let him go where he wants and I like him on the table.

You're looking at our man—studying his crooked nose. You see what neither of us has noticed until now. The hand that reaches to help you, wears a ring with a large stone. Some sort of school ring. You're thinking: Well, well, and changing your mind. As am I.

He's too good for you. Maybe might be good enough for me.

We are all, all three, the same kind of person, in one way or another. When you leave in the morning, I've seen you look to make sure there's nobody out there you might have to say hello to.

But now you talk. You think. You ask. You wonder out loud if this and that. You look down at your red and white striped shirt and wish you were wearing your usual clothes. I'm under the table wearing your brown blouse with the faint pattern of fall leaves. I look like a wrinkled up paper bag kicked under here and forgotten. The cat is down here with me purring.

It never takes long for two lonely people living in their fantasies to connect—to see all sorts of things in each other that don't exist.

They've waited for each other all their lives. They almost say so. Besides, he'd have a nice place to live if . . . if anything comes of this.

I think about that black lacy underwear. That pink silk nightie. As soon as I have a chance, I'll go get them. I might need them for myself.

But how get you moving? You're both all talk. Or *you* are, he's not talking much. Perhaps one look at the nightie might get things rolling. That'll have to be for later. Or on the other hand. . . .

I reach back to the shelf behind me and, when neither he nor you are looking, I bring out the sherry. You'll both think the other one got the bottle out.

(You do.)

You get wine glasses. You even get out your TV dinner and say you'll split it. It's turkey with stuffing. You got it special for Christmas.

Of course he says for you to eat it all, but you say you never do, anyway, so you split it.

I'm getting hungry myself. If it was just you, I would sneak a few bites but there's little enough food for the two of you. I'll have to find another way.

You both get tipsy. It doesn't take much. You hardly ever drink and it looks like he doesn't either. And I think you want to get drunk. You want something to happen as much as I do.

Every now and then I take a sip of your drinks. And on an empty stomach it takes even less. With the drone of your talk, talk, talking, I almost go to sleep.

But you're heading upstairs already.

I crawl out from under the table and climb the stairs behind you. I'm as wobbly as you are. Actually I'm wobblier. We, all three, go into your bedroom. And the cat. You push the deadbolt. He wonders why. "Aren't you alone here?"

You say, "Not exactly." And then, "I'll tell you later."

(You're right, this certainly isn't the time for a discussion about me.)

First thing I grab our sexy nightie from the drawer. I get under the bed and put it on. That's not easy, cramped up under there. For a few minutes I lose track of what's happening above me. I comb my hair as you always have it, back away from your face. I have to use my fingers and I don't have a mirror so I'm not sure how it comes out. I pinch my cheeks and bite my lips to make them redder.

The cat purrs.

I lean up to see what's going on.

Nothing much so far. Even though tipsy, he seems shy. Inexperienced. I don't think he's ever been anybody's grandfather.

(We're, all of us, all of a piece. None of us has ever been anybody's relative.)

You look pretty much passed out. Or you're pretending. Either way, it's a good time for me to make an appearance.

I crawl out from under the bed and check myself in the mirror behind them. My hair is a mess but I look good in the silky nightgown. Better than you do in your stipes and red pants. By far.

I do a little sexy dance. I say, "She's not Nora, I'm Nora. I'm the one wrote you that note."

You sit up. You were faking being drunk. You think: Now I see who you are. Now I'll get you. But you won't.

I stroke the cat. Suggestively. He purrs. (The cat, I mean.) I purr. Suggestively.

I see his eyes light up. (The man's, I mean.) Now

there'll be some action.

I say, "I don't even know your name."

He says, "Willard."

I'm on his good side because I asked, and you're not because you didn't. All this talk, talk, talk, talk, and you didn't.

You slither away, down under the bed. You feel ashamed of yourself and yet curious. You wonder: How did you ever get yourself in this position, and what to do now? But I do know what to do. I give you a kick and hand you the cat.

Willard. Willard is a little confused. But eager. More than before. He likes the nightgown and says so.

I take a good long look at him. Those bushy eyebrows. Lots of white hairs in them. I help him take off his shirt. His is not my favorite kind of chest. He does have a nice flat stomach though. (I liked that about him from the start—back when I first saw him wobbling down the street.) I look into his green/gray/tan eyes.

But what about, I love you?

I say it, "What about I love you?"

That stops him. I didn't mean to do that. I wanted to give Nora a good show. Of course it's much too soon for any sort of thing that might resemble love.

"I take that back," I say.

But it's too late. He's putting on his shirt. (It's a dressy white one. He's even wearing cufflinks engraved with W.T.)

Is it really over already?

I pick up the cat, hurry out, slam the door, and push the deadbolt on the outside, then turn back and look through the keyhole. I can see almost the whole bed.

Now look, his hands are . . . all of a sudden . . . on her and on all the right places. He knows. Maybe he actually *is* somebody's grandfather after all. And you . . . you are feeling things that make your back arch.

He tells you he loves you. *Now* he says it. He can't tell us apart. He'll love anything that comes his way.

I have what I thought I wanted . . . a good view of

something interesting for a change, except. . . .

Actually I can't see much, just his back and then your back and then his back and then yours. (How do they do that, still attached?)

Until we're all, all of us, exhausted.

I go downstairs. . . . (I like how this nightgown feels. I'm so slinky and slippery. I bump and grind just for myself.)

I make myself a peanut-butter sandwich. I feel better after eating. Things are fine.

I might leave you milk and cookies. Bring it now while you sleep so I can lock you both in again. But I don't suppose that lock will hold against two people who *really* want to get out.

I think about maybe both of you up in my crawl space. He's taller than we are. He'd not like it. I think about your job at the ice-cream factory unfolding boxes to put the ice cream in. I wouldn't mind that kind of job. You sit and daydream. I saw you. You hardly talk to anybody.

I think about how you can't prove you're you. You'll go to the police. You'll say you're you, but they'll laugh. You're clothes are all wrong for the you you used to be. They'll say, the person who's lived here all this time dresses in mouse colors. You've lived a claustrophobic life. If you'd had any friends it would be different. Besides, I can do as well as you do, unfolding boxes. I've done the same when I had jobs before I quit for this easier life. I won't be cruel. I'd never be cruel. I'll let you live in the crawl space as long as you want.

Your daydream is Willard. Or most of him, though not all. For sure his eyes. For sure his elegant slim hands and the big gold ring. You'll ask if it's a school ring.

Or one of us will. He and I will get to know each other.

Then I hear banging. And not long after that, the crash. They break open the door. It splinters where the deadbolt is. If I'd put it in the middle of the door instead of at the top, it might have held better.

By the time the door goes down I'm right outside it, watching. They run downstairs without seeing me.

I look out the window. He's leaving—hurries down the street with only one arm in his coat sleeve and it's the wrong sleeve. Other hand holds up his pants. What did you do to send him off so upset?

I open the window and call out, "Willard!" But he doesn't hear or doesn't want to. Is he trying to get away? From you or me?

What did you do to scare him so? Everything was fine when I came down to eat. But maybe getting locked in scared him. Or maybe you told him to go and never come back and you threw his coat at him as he left. Or he thinks you're me and is in love with me even though he told you he loved you.

But here you go, out the door right behind him. You have your coat on properly and your clothes all straightened up. You're wearing your red leather pants. Now you're the one calling, "Willard."

You'd not have done that before. You've changed. You'll take back your life. Everybody will make way for you now. You'll have an evil look. You'll frown. People will step off the sidewalk to let you go by.

I want for us to live as we did but you'll set traps. I'll trip on trip wires. Fall down the stairs in the middle of the night. There won't be anymore quarters lying around. You'll put a deadbolt on my door. Or better yet you'll barricade it shut with a heavy dresser. Nobody will even know there's a door there.

I made you what you are today, grand and real, but you'll lock me up up here with nothing but your mousy clothes. Your old trunks. Your dust and dark.

I dress in the worn-out clothes I wore when I came. I pack the nightgown, the black underwear. I grab a handful of quarters. I don't touch your secret stash of twenties. I pet the cat. I leave your credit cards and keys on the hall table. I don't steal.

THE PRINCE OF MULES

W HAT DO YOU KNOW from the top of a hill but the lay of the land? I can see two little towns, one on each side, and—closer—a ranch. I see cowhides all along the fences. I see skulls over the gates. I know rattlesnake skins are there, too, and maybe a skunk pelt, but I can't tell from here. There's hardly any green except in thin lines coming down from the mountains, and a couple of irrigated pastures.

And there's the irrigation ditchdigger, Blackthorn. Today he's working just below my hill. I know it's him. Who else would be out in a ditch, his clothes so black and floppy, letting himself get too hot in the middle of the day?

He has an ugly, brutal face. I don't think he's brutal but lots of people do. They distrust him because his eyebrows are too black and bushy and one eye is always off in the wrong direction. People think that eye is looking at something they can't see—something they're missing out on that might be important, or beautiful.

They say he looks like a scarecrow but what he looks like is the crow. Eye, one of them, the blackish blue of crow's eyes. Nose . . . not hooked like an eagle's, but reaching straight out. That nose says: Go somewhere. Get away. Do something else.

I see his lips moving (of course not from up here, but when I pass by down there now and then). He's always talking to his mule. I've heard tell you can talk softly to a horse but, when it comes to a mule, all you need to do is little more than mouth the words.

But it isn't as if I'm not a crow kind of person myself. And people don't like the looks of me either.

❧

My house is off alone, halfway up the hill, boulders all over my, so-called, yard. Sage. Rabbit brush. (*And* rabbits.) A skunk lives under the shed but we get along . . . so far. Same goes for the rattlesnake. So far. I probably get taken for a witch, what with a snake and a skunk for familiars. If I really was one, I'd witch away my knee pains, and I'd witch myself some money. And I'd witch myself some company. (I've lived with nothing sweeter than the rattlesnake's grin. I take as friend whatever looks at me at all.)

Blackthorn and I, we should get to know each other. Would he come up here for iced tea? Or lemonade? I don't have any beer. Come to think of it, I don't have any lemons either.

"Hello down there. Halloooo."

Can he hear me from here? I wonder if he can see me waving?

"Hallooo. Mister Blackthorn."

He sees me. He shades his eyes and looks but doesn't wave.

❧

He lives even farther up than I do. His hut is so much the color of everything else, you can hardly see it until you're practically in the doorway. I climbed up there once when he was out in the fields. I looked in the one and only window but it was so dim and dusty I couldn't see much. There was a white washbasin with a pitcher in it—both chipped. There were socks on the floor. There actually was a book—on the floor beside the socks—one of those old-fashioned, leatherbound books with gold lettering. I couldn't read the title. I was surprised and pleased to see he actually had a real book.

But the shed for the mule—now that was spic and span. Smelled sweet of straw and hay and mule. Smelled so good I took a chance and lay down there for a while.

I call again. "Hallooooo."

Again he looks up, but just as he did before, he goes right back to digging. He's got to be tired and thirsty. Suppose I hold up a big glass of iced tea? Suppose I had a pail of water for the mule?

I go in, change my blouse to a cream colored one (mule nose color actually) with lace around the neck, and come back out with a pitcher and a pail. I hold them over my head.

"Halloooow!"

Finally!

When the time comes to say my name, what would be unusual and romantic and make him remember it? *And* me?

So he and his mule come all the way up here, two switchbacks and then a long sideways.

He lets the mule drink first. (Of course!) He calls her sweetheart. How he does sweet talk that mule! "Come sweetheart. Come, Penny, drink." (When has anybody ever called me sweetheart? I think and think, but I'm thinking, Never.)

He says she came with the name Bad Penny, but he calls her Pennyroyal.

It looks like that's all he's going to say. Sometimes people who don't talk much like to have other people chatter away so they don't have to think about talking, they don't even have to listen; and yet others like silence around them to match their own.

"Do these ditches need you? Every single day like this?"

"Without me and Penny everything would be as dry as it is right here." His good eye takes it all in: me, my tin pitcher, my boulders. . . . The other eye is off at its own secret spot. I can tell he's never noticed me before, even after all those times I was walking back and forth in front of his ditch whenever he was working near my hill.

"Did you ever think of going someplace else?"

"I've been elsewhere."

He drinks my whole pitcherful right out of the pitcher and without stopping. I should have had as much for him as for the mule.

I like his eyebrows. I even like his eye that roves off seeing . . . God knows what visions.

By now I can tell what my name should be. I say, "I'm Molly," so as to be more mule. Though, on second thought, perhaps I should have said Jenny so I could be Jenny to his Jack. I wonder if his first name *is* Jack.

How to keep him here a little while longer? "Could you open this jar?" (He could.) "Could you move this heavy box for me?" (Of course.) "And I can't reach this shelf."

He does all the things and with an old crow's grace. An old crow's flashing eye.

I feel so good I want to say, Sweetheart, to something myself, except Penny's the one getting all the caresses. Does she need so many when there's others (not so far away) who haven't had any? As to looks, she's nothing special, just the general mule color, dark with a cream colored nose, but she's sleek and shiny, which is more than I can say about him. Or myself.

Perhaps, in that wandering eye, Penny is a beautiful woman as pale all over as the star on her forehead, her hair the same black/brown of the turkey vulture feathers he has in his hat.

What *is* he seeing with that off-kilter eye? Suppose he looked at me through that? What would I turn into? But perhaps, for starters, I need to become more mulish. Mules always know what they want to do and when. They're never wishy-washy. They know what's best for everybody. I suppose he depends on her for his own safety. I'm afraid I don't have that knack.

My ravens quack, quack, quack around us. Something else is going, "Tweet, tweet, churrrrr. Tweet, tweet, churrrrr." He lifts his head—points his going-somewhere nose and listens like a poet. Who'd have thought?

"Could I have a ditch? One connected to the arroyo just in case there's ever a little bit of water in it?" (There hasn't been any water in it since I came here.) "It wouldn't have to be long or deep. I'll pay."

I seem to have decided (without deciding) on too much talking though I'm not yet committed to it *completely*. I keep silent as I hand him more tea. I think of all the things I'm not saying, as: Take me to your shack, old crow man. Or take me even farther up, to the mountain lion's den. I saw a place up there where the grass was matted in a cozy circle. I saw the scat.

What I do say is: "When I die I had always wanted to come back—if there's going to be any coming back to it—as a raven. I had wanted to be smart and cocky, but now that I see Penny, I think, perhaps, mule is better."

What I don't say is, who ever caresses a raven?

What I do say is: "I have stones as if instead of trees. All my shade is from boulders. I'm surprised anything grows here at all but some things find a way. They get a toehold. Like I do."

I don't say: My stones are warm and motherly after a day in the sun and I lean against their big round bellies every evening. They're warm well into the night.

He has looked at me again. One of his fleeting glances that slip sideways and down before you know you've been looked at.

What I do say is, "I thought I heard a stream or maybe it's leaves blowing. I heard another, tweet, tweet, churr from some other place entirely. And it's cool somewhere not far from here." I spread my arms, the better to feel the breeze. "Admit it. There's another world somewhere, all shiny and sweet smelling. Not a bit like here."

He spreads his arms, too, but to show my hill and my view. "Why do you want to see more than this right here, the gray fox colors of the underbrush, and, not far, the fox herself and her kits."

Spoken like a poet. And what more *do* I want than the warm bellies of the granite? And there *is* a tree, one, and more up where he is.

But I think there *is* a world of the other eye, and in it he would be the wiry black prince of mules. And he would have shaved in that world. His hat would smooth itself out and clean itself up and the turkey vulture feathers would become the feathers of a hawk. No, eagle.

I say, "I saw sparkles. Diamond shapes, all different colors and all in a row. I heard swishing sounds as if a stream or of poplar leaves in the wind. I heard wind chimes. I felt how cool. I shivered. Look how I shiver. I saw. . . . I thought I saw Penny. She was wearing a nightgown sort of thing. Even now your other eye is glistening. I see tears on that cheek."

I step forward to wipe the tear but he jerks back.

"My other eye sees nothing."

"And does the nothing have a light-blue cast?"

"There's no other place than here."

"I don't believe it."

"Believe what you will, people always do, and they like the odd and scandalous and fantastic better than the real."

"What about Pennyroyal?"

"She is as you see."

But I know better.

Except now he's on his way down—*already* on his way, back to his ditch.

"It's too hot!" I'm screeching it. Then I screech again. "Dangerous to work in such heat!" (What kind of bird is that, that screeches so? None I ever knew.) "A man of your age. . . ." Screech, screech.

He's going. He's down. And he didn't say if he'd dig me

a ditch or not.

But I know happiness *is* possible because I don't want a lot of it. How sweet it would be to sleep in the hay with Penny. That's not much to ask.

Like his nose says, I'll go forward, do something, go elsewhere. I will know what I want. I will become more mule.

I go back in and pack up my nightgown and a snack. (The nightgown might be important.) I sit on one of my rocks and wait until I see Blackthorn and Penny leave the ditch. (She doesn't even have a lead rope. She follows him home on her own. I would, too. I *will*.)

❧

I wait until it's almost dark and then I take my bundle and climb up into the piñons. There's a light in his shack, but dim. No doubt an oil lamp or candles. I peek in. Blackthorn is at the little table, leaning over it, side view. (I *do* like that going-someplace look of his nose.)

With that lamplight I can see more than I could before. Things are nicer than I thought, though I see sandy dust all over everything. (I could clean that up in no time.) There's a patchwork quilt on the cot, Secret Star pattern. There's a humpbacked trunk. Hard to put anything down on top of that but there's not only a couple of dirty shirts lying across it, but a tin cup balanced at the top of the curve. I hope the cup's empty. The washbowl and pitcher look even more chipped and cracked in this light, and dirty socks are on the floor again—or still. Maybe a couple more pairs. They need darning. I'll do that.

Then I notice I'm on the side of his rambling eye and it's rambling right over to the window—to me. I don't know what he sees, but there's no reaction. It's as if that eye *is* blind, but maybe it's that he's seeing wonderful things and wouldn't be paying attention to me anyway.

And now he has that poet's look of listening. Have I made a noise?

The odd eye is still right on me. It glistens in the lamp light. His good eye was crow-blue-black. This one is *light* blue.

I think of clouds tinged pink, rainbows of course . . . balconies, gazebos, long white gauzy gowns that blow in the wind, raven hair . . . "tresses," as they say, also blowing. And Blackthorn. . . . In the world of that blue eye, he would wear clothes that fit him better, though they'd still be black. Penny would have a long courtly nose (as she already has) and her tresses would make her face look all the more narrow, but what makes somebody beautiful? Not their nose. Not perfect teeth. Not big caramel-colored eyes. (She does have that.)

∾

"Harriet?" Now it's his good eye which is turned towards me. "Harriet?"

How did he know my real name? Another sure sign of . . . well, several things. If he knows my name then for sure there *is* another world out there somewhere.

I hear wind. Branches squeak as they brush against the roof of the shack. I feel the evening breeze. Or is that in that other place?

He says, "Enter."

Enter what? Does he mean into that other land? And how? Since I don't know how to go there, for now, and though I'm right by the door, I just step through the little window. It's small and high, but I step through just as though it was easy—except I fall when I land on the other side. I'm down by his knees. I dare to touch his ankle. He's not wearing any shoes or socks so I touch bare skin. I look up into his eyes . . . eye, that is. You have to pick which one you want to look into.

"Please get up."

But his ankle is warm and damp. I haven't touched skin-to-skin with anybody for longer than I can remember. I lay my cheek across his instep. It smells of ditch.

"*Please* get up."

I kiss his foot.

But I'm way, way, way. . . . I'm way. . . .

❧

. . . on a hill holding the ankle of (of course!) a black stallion. (Who would be holding the ankle of a gelding!) There's moonlight. There's a breeze. Blue-black clouds scoot across the sky. It's a witch kind of land. Scary. I knew it would be. I knew *all* this.

The stallion paws with the hoof I'm not holding, impatient. I know he means, "For Heaven's sake get *up*! I asked you to before."

I do. I should at least be wearing something flowing so I'd match the setting. (I knew I'd need my nightgown, but where is it now?) But I'm dressed as I was, lacy mule-nose-colored shirt and loose old lady jeans. For sure, here, I'm no younger than I was in the other place. I can feel that in my knees as I get up.

He shakes his head, hard, up and down, mane flying, impatient still. (In this world it's the good eye, the black one, that seems odd.) He walks away, looking back at me. I follow. The grass here is soft against my legs just as I knew it would be, not like my grass, all scratchy and in clumps. Not far away I hear water running. It sounds like a small stream, nothing of the flash flood about it. He, the stallion, comes to a rock and stops beside it as though I should use it as a mounting block.

I wonder if, in this world, I might know how to ride. Maybe know how to stay on even if bareback with nothing to hang on to but the mane. And how do you steer?

I mount. Now I'm glad I'm not wearing something flowing. Except, without a skirt and scarves, there'll be nothing to blow out behind us as we gallop. Only his mane and tail, not my hair. It's much too short. And would gray hair count anyway?

He starts away at an easy trot—but I've already fallen

off the other side. We go back to the mounting-stone. This time I get a better grip on the mane. I hadn't thought his back would be so slippery and bounce so.

There will be a castle. Or perhaps a smaller cozy summer castle (I'd like that) where they (*we*) pretend to be ordinary people. Pennyroyal, the princess all in white. Her beauty is in the look in her eye. (Everybody says so.) And in the tilt of her head. There is no kinder princess. (Everybody says so.) She does nothing but smile. But her voice is a little like mine was when I screeched. (Now I know that sound I made, birds don't do that, it's mule.) She smiles. At me. She calls me Sweetheart. (*Everybody* calls me Sweetheart!)

I curtsey. Sort of a curtsey. It isn't until I try it that I realize I don't know how. Where do the arms go? How low is low enough?

I'm thinking Penny is his little sister so I could be his wife. That is, if he ever can, in *this* world, *not* be a stallion. Perhaps all it takes is my kiss (like with frogs) but on his lips, not just his ankle where I kissed him before. Was it that kiss that started all this? That turned him horse in the first place?

❧

But they don't need any more princesses here. *Everybody* can't be one. What they need is. . . .

❧

When I leaned my cheek against his foot back in his cabin, I'd thought how nice it would be if I could clean up the shack, scrub and dust, do the dirty socks and shirts, darn, wash the dishes. Pull down hay for Penny. Sleep in the sweet-smelling shed. Be his little helping-elf. Or anything he wants me to be. I even thought: When can I start?

But here, I've already started—shoveling out the stables. "Sweetheart, could you kindly go. . . ." And I was even stroked a bit before I go there.

Here . . . even here . . . what they need is a scullery maid. I'm to sleep in the stables. It's not at all the same as it would have been if I'd been set to clean Penny's stall and sleep with her and clean his shack up, up there under the piñons.

How to get out of it? The stallion must know. If I could get him to take the bit—I'd bloody up his mouth if I had to—to make him go back to that hill where the entrance to all this might be. *Maybe* might be.

Or if I could wake up and it would all have been a dream (it looks like a dream and feels like a dream) and I would be there, my cheek still on his foot. If that happened, I'd not kiss, as I did, I'd bite.

Or if I could go into his stall and bite his foot *now* and be instantly transported back to his shack. (I do creep in to try that and he heehaws as if he was a mule.)

Or what if I could put out his eye? But which one! That's important. If the wrong one, then I might be here forever.

And all this after I gave him water from my tank. It isn't as if water grows on trees around here—back there I mean.

If I ever do get back, I'll have to end up hugging the warm rock bellies like I used to. I'll have to make do with whatever slithers by. But I don't care anymore. I'll wave at crow or snake or sweet gray fox. . . .

Those townspeople were right. Jack Blackthorn! I should have known all this (as they did) from his name and his off-kilter eye and from those bushy eyebrows.

BOYS

WE NEED A NEW batch of boys. Boys are so foolhardy, impetuous, reckless, rash. They'll lead the way into smoke and fire and battle. I've seen one of my own sons, aged twelve, standing at the top of the cliff shouting, daring the enemy. You'll never win a medal for being too reasonable.

We steal boys from anywhere. We don't care if they come from our side or theirs. They'll forget soon enough which side they used to be on, if they ever knew. After all, what does a seven-year-old know? Tell them this flag of ours is the best and most beautiful, and that we're the best and smartest, and they believe it. They like uniforms. They like fancy hats with feathers. They like to get medals. They like flags and drums and war cries.

Their first big test is getting to their beds. You have to climb straight up to the barracks. At the top you have to cross a hanging bridge. They've heard rumors about it. They know they'll have to go home to mother if they don't do it. They all do it.

You should see the look on their faces when we steal them. It's what they've always wanted. They've seen our fires along the hills. They've seen us marching back and forth across our flat places. When the wind is right, they've heard the horns that signal our getting up and going to bed and they've gotten up and gone to bed with our sounds or those of our enemies across the valley.

In the beginning they're a little bit homesick (you can hear them smothering their crying the first few nights) but most have anticipated their capture and look forward to it. They love to belong to us instead of to the mothers.

If we'd let them go home they'd strut about in their uniforms and the stripes of their rank. I know because I remember when I first had my uniform. I was wishing my mother and my big sister could see me. When I was taken, I fought, but just to show my courage. I was happy to be stolen—happy to belong, at long last, to the men.

Once a year in summer we go down to the mothers and copulate in order to make more warriors. We can't ever be completely sure which of the boys is ours and we always say that's a good thing, for then they're all ours and we care about them equally, as we should. We're not supposed to have family groups. It gets in the way of combat. But every now and then, it's clear who the father is. I know two of my sons. I'm sure they know that I, the colonel, am their father. I think that's why they try so hard. I know them as mine because I'm a small, ugly man. I know many must wonder how someone like me got to be a colonel.

(We not only steal boys from either side but we copulate with either side. When I go down to the villages, I always look for Una.)

To die for your tribe is to live forever. That's written over our headquarters entrance. Under it, Never forget. We know we mustn't forget but we suspect maybe we have. Some of us feel that the real reasons for the battles have been lost. No doubt but that there's hate, so we and they commit more atrocities in the name of the old ones, but how it all began is lost to us.

We've not only forgotten the reasons for the conflict, but we've also forgotten our own mothers. Inside our barracks, the walls are covered with mother jokes and mother pictures. Mother bodies are soft and tempting. "Pillows," we call them. "Nipples" and "pillows." And we insult each other by calling ourselves the same.

The valley floor is full of women's villages. One every fifteen miles or so. On each side are mountains. The enemy's, at the far side, are called The Purples. Our mountains are called The Snows. The weather is worse in our mountains than in theirs. We're proud of that. We sometimes call ourselves The Hailstones or The Lightnings. We think the hailstones harden us up. The enemy doesn't have as many caves over on their side. We always tell the boys they were lucky to be stolen by us and not those others.

When I was first taken, our mothers came up to the caves to get us back. That often happens. Some had weapons. Laughable weapons. My own mother was there, in the front of course. She probably organized the whole thing, her face, red and twisted with resolve. She came straight at me. I was afraid of her. We boys fled to the back of the barracks and our squad leader stood in front of us. Other men covered the doorway. It didn't take long for the mothers to retreat. None were hurt. We try never to do them any harm. We need them for the next crop of boys.

Several days later my mother came again by herself —sneaked up by moonlight. Found me by the light of the night lamp. She leaned over my sleeping mat and breathed on my face. At first I didn't know who it was. Then I felt breasts against my chest and I saw the glint of a hummingbird pin I recognized. She kissed me. I was petrified. (Had I been a little older I'd have known how to choke and kick to the throat. I might have killed her before I realized it was my mother.) What if she took me from my squad? Took away my uniform? (By then I had a red and blue jacket with gold buttons. I had already learned to shoot. Something I'd always wanted to do. I was the first of my group to get a sharpshooters medal. They said I was a natural. I was trying hard to make up for my small size.)

The night my mother came she lifted me in her arms. There, against her breasts, I thought of all the pillow jokes. I yelled. My comrades, though no older than I and only a little larger, came to my aid. They picked up whatever weapon was handy, mostly their boots. (Thank goodness we had not received our daggers yet.) My mother wouldn't hit out at the boys. She let them batter at her. I wanted her to hit back, to run, to save herself. After she finally did run, I found I had bitten my lower lip. In times of stress I'm inclined to do that. I have to watch out. When you're a colonel, it's embarrassing to be found with blood on your chin.

So now, off to steal boys. We're a troop of older boys and younger men. The oldest maybe twenty-two, half my age. I think of them all as boys, though I would never call them boys to their faces. I'm in charge. My son, Hob, he's seventeen now, is with us.

But we no sooner creep down to the valley than we see things have changed since last year. The mothers have put up a wall. They've built themselves a fort.

I immediately change our plans. I decide this will be copulation day, not boys day. Good military strategy: Always be ready for a quick change of plan.

The minute I think this, I think Una. This is her town. My men look happy, too. This is not only easier, but lots more fun than herding a new crop of boys.

Last time I came down at copulation time I found her—or she found me, she usually does. She's a little old for copulation day, but I didn't want anybody but her. After copulation, I did things for her, repaired a roof leak, fixed a broken table leg. . . . Then I took her over again, though it wasn't needed, and caused my squad to have to wait for me. Got me a lot of lewd remarks, but I felt extraordinarily happy anyway.

Sometimes on boys night I wonder, what if I stole Una along with boys? What if I dressed her as a boy and brought her to some secret hiding place on our side of the mountain? There are lots of unused caves. Once our armies occupied them all, but that was long ago. Both us and our enemies seem to be dwindling. Every year there are fewer and fewer suitable boys.

Una always seems glad to see me even though I'm ugly and small. (My size is a disadvantage for a soldier, though less so now that I have rank, but the ugliness . . . that's how I can tell which are my sons . . . small, ugly boys, both of them. Too bad for them. But I've managed well even so, all the way up to colonel.)

Una was my first. I was her first, too. I felt sorry for her, having to have me for her beginning to be a woman. We were little more than children. We hardly knew what we were doing or how to do it. Afterwards she cried. I felt like crying myself but I had learned not to. Not just learned it with the squad, but I had learned it even before they took me from my mother. I wanted to be taken. I roamed far out into the scrub, waiting for them to come and get me.

The pain in my hip started when I was one of those boys. It wasn't from a wound in a skirmish with the enemy, but from a fight among ourselves. Our leaders were happy when we fought each other. We'd have gotten soft and lazy if we didn't. I keep my mouth shut about my injury. I kept my mouth shut even when I got it. I thought if they knew I could be so easily hurt they'd send me back. Later, I thought if they knew about it, I might not be allowed to come on our raids. Later still I thought I might not be able to be a colonel. I don't let myself limp though sometimes that makes me more breathless than I should be. So far it doesn't seem as if anybody's noticed.

We regroup. I say, "Fellow nipples and fellow pillows. . . ." Everybody laughs. "When have they ever stopped men? Look how womanish the walls are. They'll crumble as we climb." I scrape at a part with the tip of my cane. (As a colonel, I'm allowed to have a cane if I wish instead of a swagger stick.)

We're not sure if the women want to stop copulation day or boy gathering day. We hope it's the latter.

Boost up the smallest boy with a rope on hooks. The rest of us follow.

I used to be that smallest boy. I always went first and highest. Times like this I was glad for my size. I got medals for that. I don't wear any of them. I like playing at being one of the boys. Being small and being a colonel is a good example for some. If they knew about my bum leg I'd be an even better example of how far you can get with disabilities.

We scale the walls and drop into the edges of a vegetable garden. We walk carefully around tomatoes and strawberry plants, squash and beans. After that, raspberry bushes tear at our pants and untie our high-tops as we go by. There's a row of barbed wire just beyond the raspberries. Easy to push down.

I feel sad that the women want to keep us out so badly. I wonder, does Una want me not to come? Except they know we're as determined as mothers. At least I am when it comes to Una.

Una has always been nice to me. I often wonder why she likes me. I can understand somebody liking me now that I'm a colonel with silver on my epaulets, and a silver handled cane, but she liked me when I was nothing but a runty boy. She's small, too. I always think Una and I fit together except for one thing, she's beautiful.

We swarm in, turn, each to our favorite place, the younger ones to what's left over, usually other young ones. But then here we are, swarming back again, into their central square, the place with the well, and stone benches, and their one and only tree. Around the tree are the graves of babies. The benches are the mourning benches. We sit on them or on the ground. There's nobody here, not a single woman nor girl nor baby.

Then there's the sound of shooting. We move from the central square—we can't see anything from there. We hide behind the houses at the edges of the gardens. Our enemy stands along the top of the wall. We're ambushed. We flop down. We have no rifles with us and only two pistols, mine and my lieutenant's. This wasn't supposed to be a skirmish. We have our daggers, of course.

Those along the wall don't seem to be very good shots. I raised my pistol. I'm thinking to show them what a good shot really is. But my lieutenant yells, "Stop! Don't shoot. It's mothers!"

Women all along the wall! And with guns. Hiding under wall-colored shields. Whoever heard of such a thing.

They shoot, but a lot are missing, I think on purpose. After all, we may be the enemy, but we're the fathers of many of their girls and many of them. I wonder which one is Una.

The women are angrier than we thought. Perhaps they're tired of losing their boys to us and to the other side. I wouldn't put it past them not to be on any side whatsoever.

Our boys begin to yell their war cry but in a half hearted way. But then . . . one shot . . . a real shot this time. Good shot, too. One wonders how a woman could have done it. One wonders if it was a man who taught her. The boys are stunned. To think that one of their mothers or one of their sisters would shoot to kill. This is real. We hadn't thought they'd harm us any more than we ever really harm them.

It was my lieutenant they killed. One bloodless shot to the head. For that boy's sake I'm glad at least no pain. He was wearing his ceremonial hat. I wasn't wearing mine. I never liked that fancy heavy hat. I suppose they really wanted to kill me, but had to take second best since they couldn't tell which one I was. Una would know which one was me.

The boys scatter—back to the center square with its mourning tree. The women can't see them back there. I stay to check on the dead lieutenant and to get his dagger and pistol. Then I limp back to where the boys are waiting for me to tell them what to do. Limp. I relax into it. I don't care who sees. I haven't exactly given up, though perhaps I have when it comes to my future. I'll most likely be demoted. To be captured by women. . . . All twenty of us. If I can't get out of this in an efficient and capable way, there goes my career.

I hope they have the sense to come rescue us with a large group. They'll have to make a serious effort. I hope they don't try to fight and at the same time try to save the women for future use.

But then we hear shooting again and we look out from behind the huts near the wall and see the women have turned their guns outwards. At first we think it's us, come to rescue us, but it's not. That's not our battle cry, not our drum beats. . . . We can't see from behind the walls so some of us go up on the roofs. There's no danger, all the rifles are facing outwards, but our boys would have braved the roof without a word, as they always do.

It's not our red and blue banners. It's their ugly green and white. It's the enemy come to take advantage of our capture. We wish the women would get out of the way and let us go so we could fight for ourselves. Those women are breaking every rule of battle. They're lying flat along their wall. Nobody can get a fair shot at them.

It goes on and on. We get tired of watching and retreat to the square. We reconnoiter food from the kitchens. We eat better than we usually do. The food is so good we wish the women would let up a bit so we can enjoy it without that racket. Where did they get all these weapons? They must have found our ammunition caves and those of our enemy, too.

The women do a pretty good job. By nightfall our enemy has fled back into their mountains and the women are still on top of their wall. It looks as if they're going to spend the night up there. It's a wide wall. Not as badly built as I told the boys it was.

We find beds for ourselves, all of them better than our usual sleeping pads. I go to Una's hut and lie where I had hoped to have a copulation.

Cats prowl and yowl. All sorts of things live with the women. Goats wander the streets and come in any house they want to. All the animals expect food everywhere. Like the women, our boys are soft hearted. They feed every creature that comes by. I don't let on that I do too.

This whole thing makes me sad. Worried. If I could just have Una in my arms, I might be able to sleep. I have a "day dream" of her creeping in to me in the middle of the night. I wouldn't even care if we had a copulation or not.

In the morning boys climb to the roofs again to see what's up. They describe women lying under shields all along the walls and they can see some of the enemy lying dead away from the walls. I need to climb up and see for myself. Besides it's good for the boys to see me taking the same chances they do.

I send the boys off and I take their place. I look down on the women along the wall. I see several rifles pointed at me. I stand like a hero. I dare them to shoot. I take all the time I want. I see wall sections less crowded with women. I take out my notebook (no leader is ever without one) and draw a diagram. I take my time until I have the whole wall mapped out.

I could take out my pistol and threaten them. I could shoot one but it wouldn't be very manly to take advantage of my high point. Were they men I'd do it. But then they do the unmanly thing. They shoot me. My leg. My good leg. I go down, flat on the roof. At first I feel nothing but the shock . . . as if I'd been hit with a hammer. All I know is I can't stand up. Then I see blood.

Though they're on the wall, they're lower. They can't see me as long as I keep down. I crawl to the edge where boys help me. They carry me back to Una's bed. I feel I'm about to pass out or throw up and I become aware that I've soiled myself. I don't want the boys to see. I've always been a source of strength and inspiration in spite of or because of my size.

One of those boys is Hob, come to help me, my arm across his shoulders. I lean in pain but keep my groans to myself.

"Sir? Colonel?"

"I'm fine. Will be. Go."

I wish I could ask him if he really is my son. They say sometimes the women know and tell the boys.

"Don't you want us to . . ."

"No. Go. Now. And shut the door."

They leave just in time. I throw up over the side of the bed. I lie back—Una's pillow all sweated up not to mention what I've done to her quilt.

Una can make potions for pain. I wish I knew which, of the herbs hanging from her ceiling, might help me. But I'd not be able to reach them anyway.

I lie, half conscious, for I don't know how long. Every time I sit up to examine my leg, I feel nausea again and have to lie back. I wonder if I'll ever be able to lead a charge or a raid for boys or a copulation day. And I always thought, when I became a general (and lately I felt sure I'd be one) maybe I'd find out what we're fighting for—beyond, that is, the usual rhetoric we use to make ourselves feel superior. Now I suppose I'll never know the real reasons.

The boys knock. I rouse myself and say, "Come." Try, that is. At first my voice won't sound out at all and then it sounds more like a groan than a word. The boys tell me the women have called down from the wall. They want to send in a spokesman. The boys want to let him in and then hold him hostage so that we'll all be let out safely.

I tell them the women will probably send in a woman.

That bothers the boys. They must have had torture or killing in mind but now they look worried.

"Tell them yes," I say.

It must smell terrible in here. I even smell terrible to myself, and it's uncomfortable sitting in my own mess. I prop myself up as best I can. I hope I can keep to my senses. I hope I don't throw up in the middle of it. I put my dagger, unsheathed, under the pillow.

At first I think the boys were right, it's a man, of course a man. Where would they have found him, and is he from our side or theirs? That's important. I can't tell by the colors. He's all in tan and gray. He's not wearing any stripes at all so I can't tell his rank. He stands, at ease. More than at ease, utterly relaxed, and in front of a colonel.

But then . . . I can't believe it, it's Una. I should have known. Dressed as a man down to the boots. I have such a sense of relief and after that joy. Everything will be all right now.

I tell the boys to get out and shut the door.

I reach for her, but the look on her face stops me.

"You shot me in the leg on purpose, didn't you! My good leg!"

"I meant to shoot the bad one."

She opens all the windows, and the door again, too, and shoos the boys away.

"Let me see."

She's gentle. As I knew she'd be.

"I'll get the bullet out, but first I'll clean you up." She hands me leaves to chew for pain.

As she leans, so close above me, her hair falls out of her cap and brushes my face, gets in my mouth as it does when we have copulation day. I reach to touch her breast but she pushes me away.

I should kill her for the glory of it . . . the leader of the women. I'd not be thought a failure then. I'd be made a general in no time.

But, as she pulls away the soiled quilts, she finds my dagger first thing. She puts it in the drawer with her kitchen knives.

I think again how . . . (and we all know, only too well) how love is a dangerous thing and can spoil the best of plans. Even as I think it, I want to spoil the very plans I think of. I mean if she's the leader then I could deal with her right now, as she leans over me—even without my dagger. They may be good shots, but can they wrestle a man? Even a wounded one?

"I chose you because I thought, of all of them, you might listen."

"You know I won't ever be let come down to copulation day again."

"Don't go back then. Stay here and copulate."

"I have often thought to bring you up to the mountain dressed as a man. I have a place all picked out."

"Stay here. Let *everybody* stay here and be as women."

I can't answer such a thing. I can't even think about it.

"But then what else do you know except how to be a colonel?"

She washes me, changes the bed, and throws the bed clothes and my clothes out the door. Then she gets the bullet out. I'm half out of my head from the leaves she had me chew so the pain is dulled. She bandages me, covers me with a clean blanket, puts her lips against my cheek for a moment.

Then stands up, legs apart. She looks like one of our boys getting ready to prove himself. "We'll not stand for this anymore," she says. "It has to end and we'll end it, if not one way, then another."

"But this is how it's always been."

"You could be our spokesman."

How can she even suggest such a thing. "Pillows," I say. "Spokesman for the nipples."

Goodness knows what the mothers are capable of. They never stick to any rules.

"If the answer is no, we'll not have anymore boy babies. You can come down and copulate all you want but there'll be no boys. We'll kill them."

"You wouldn't. You couldn't. Not you, Una."

"Have you noticed how there are fewer and fewer boys? Many have already done it."

But I'm in too much pain and dizzy from the leaves she gave me, to think clearly. She sees that. She sits beside me, takes my hand. "Just rest," she says. How can I rest with such ideas in my head? "But the rules."

"Hush. Women don't care about rules. You know that."

"Come back with me." I pull her down against me. This time she lets me. How good it feels to have us chest to chest, my arms around her. "I have a secret place. It's not a hard climb to get there."

She pulls back. "Colonel, sir!"

"Please don't call me that."

Then I say . . . what we're not allowed to say or even think. It's a mother/child thing, not to be said between a man and a woman. I say, "I love you."

She leans back and looks at me. Then wipes at my chin. "Try not to bite your lip like that."

"It doesn't matter anymore."

"It does to me."

"I liked. . . . I like. . . ." I already used the other word, why not yet again. "I love copulation day only when with you."

I wonder if she feels the same about me. I wish I dared ask her. I wonder if my son. . . . Is Hob hers and mine together? I've always hoped he was. She's made no gesture towards him. She hasn't even looked at him any more than any other boy. This would have been his first copulation day had the women not built their wall.

"Rest," she says. "We'll discuss later."

"Is it just us? Or are you saying the same thing to the enemy? They could win the war like that. It would be your fault."

"Stop thinking."

"What if no more boys on either side, ever?"

"What if?"

She gives me more of those leaves to chew. They're bitter. I was in too much pain to notice that the first time. I feel even sleepier right away.

I dream I'm the last of all the boys. Ever. I have to get somewhere in a hurry, but there's a wall so high I'll never get over it. Beside, my legs are not there at all. I'm nothing but a torso. Women watch me. Women, off across the valley floor as far as I can see and none will help. There's nothing to do but lie there and give the war cry.

I wake shouting and with Una holding me down. Hob is there, helping her. Other boys are in the doorway looking worried.

I've thrown the blanket and the pillow to the floor and now I seem to be trying to throw myself out of bed. Una has a long scratch across her cheek. I must have done that.

"Sorry. Sorry."

I'm still as if in a dream. I pull Una down against me. Hold her hard and then I reach out for Hob, too. My poor ugly boy. I ask the unaskable. "Tell me, is Hob mine and yours together?"

Hob looks shocked that I would ask such a thing, as well he should. Una pulls away and gets up. She answers as if she was one of the boys. "Colonel, sir, how can you, of all people, ask a thing like that." Then she throws my own words back at me. "This is how it's always been."

"Sorry. Sorry."

"Oh, for Heaven's sake stop being so *sorry!*"

She shoos the boys from the doorway but she lets Hob stay. Together they rearrange the bed. Together she and Hob make broth for me and food for themselves. Hob seems at home here. It's true, I'm sure. This is our son.

But I suppose all this yearning, all this wondering, is due to the leaves Una had me chew. It's not the real me. I'll not pay any attention to myself.

But there's something else. I didn't get a good look at my leg yet, but it feels like a serious wound. If I can't climb up to our stronghold, I'll not ever be able to go home. I shouldn't, even so, and though my career is in a shambles . . . . I shouldn't let myself be lured into staying here as a copulator for the rest of my life. I can't think of anything more dishonorable. I should send Hob back to the citadel to report on what's happened and to get help. If he was found trying to escape, would Una let the women kill him?

I try to get Hob alone so I can whisper his orders to him. Only when Una goes out to the privy do I get the chance. "Get back to the citadel. Cross the wall tonight. There's no moon." I show him my map and where I think there are fewer women. I want to tell him to take care, but we don't ever say such things.

In the morning I tell Una to tell my leaders to come in to me. I'm in pain, in a sweat, my beard is itchy. I ask Una to clean me up. She treats me as a mother would. Back when my mother did it, I pulled away. I wouldn't let her get close to me. I especially wouldn't let her hug or kiss me. I wanted to be a soldier. I wanted nothing to do with mother things.

All the boys are looking scruffy. We take pride in our cleanliness, in shaving everyday, in our brush cuts, and our enemy is as spic and span as we are. I hope they don't launch an offensive today and see us so untidy.

I'm glad to see Hob isn't with them.

I find it hard to rouse myself to my usual humor. I say, "Pillows, nipples," but I'm too uncomfortable to play at being one of the boys.

I'd prefer to recuperate some, but the boys are restless already. I can't be thinking of myself. We'll storm the wall. I show them the map. I point out the less guarded spots. I grab Una. Both her wrists. "Men, we'll need a battering ram."

Wood isn't easy to get out here on the valley floor. This is a desert except along the streams, but every village has one tree in the center square that they've nurtured along. As here, baby's graves are always around it. In other villages, most are cottonwood, but this one is oak. It's so old I wouldn't be surprised if it hadn't been here since before the village. I think the village was built up around it later.

"Chop the tree. Ram the wall." I tell them. "Go back to the citadel. Don't wait around for me. Tell the generals never to come here again, neither for boys nor for copulation. Tell them I'm of no use to us anymore."

The women won't be able to shoot at the boys chopping it down. It's hidden from all parts of the wall.

When they hear the chopping, the women begin to ululate. Our boys stop chopping, but only for a moment. I hear them begin again with even more vigor.

Here beside me Una ululates, too. She struggles against me but I hang on.

"How could you? That's the tree of dead boys."

I let go.

"All the babies buried there are boys. Some are yours."

I can't let this new knowledge color my thinking. I have to think of the safety of my boys. "Let us go, then."

"Tell them to stop."

"Would you let us go for the sake of a tree?"

"We would."

I give the order.

The women move away from a whole section of the wall, they even provide their ladders. I tell the boys to go. There's no way they could carry me back and no way I could ever climb to the citadel again.

No sooner are the boys gone, even to the last tootle of the fifes, the last triumphant drum beat. . . . (We always march home as though victorious whether victorious or not.) Hearing them go, I can't help but groan, though not from pain this time. No sooner have the mothers come down from the wall, but that I hear, ululating again. Una stamps in to me.

"What now?"

"It's Hob. Your enemy. . . . *Your* enemy has dropped him off at the edge of your foothills."

I can see it on her face.

"He's dead."

"Of course he's dead. You are all as good as dead."

She blames me for Hob. "I blame myself."

"I hate you. I hate you all."

I don't believe we'll be seeing many boys anymore. I would warn us if I was able, I would be the spokesman, though I don't suppose I'll ever have the chance.

"What will the women do with me?"

"You were always kind. I'll not be any less to you."

What am I good for? What use am I but to stay here as the father of females? All those small, ugly, black-haired girls. . . . I suppose all of them biting their lower lips until they bleed.

THE DOCTOR

HE DATES HIS THIRD WIFE often but she'll not come back to live with him. Even before it got this bad she said he'd have to clean out this place first. Have to get new couches not so clawed and peed on. Use a lot of spray for the smell. But there's no way to clean it up now without burning it down.

She left him five years ago. She had good reasons, lots more than just this mess. One was, he was a partying person and she wasn't. (Of course if she came back now there couldn't be any parties anyway, at least not for a long while of cleaning up.) And of course you never can know people's reasons for leaving—nor for coming back.

The doctor has rugged sexy good looks. He's still attractive even though in his seventies and even though he broke his back which left him with a crunched-down look. He used to be six feet three but now he's only six feet. As a young man he had dislocated and broken his fingers so often they look terrible now, crooked and with swollen joints. One wonders how he can be a surgeon, thread his needles, and tie the fancy little knots anymore.

The house is a huge Victorian with a front stairway and a back stairway, five bedrooms not counting the maid's room, two upstairs bathrooms and one downstairs (only one toilet still works, but the doctor is alone, he doesn't need more than one). The front parlor is all bay windows and the back parlor is all wood paneling.

There's empty fields behind the house and little patches of forest on each side. Sometimes deer come in to the doctor's back yard.

The third wife said if he'd clean the place up even a little bit she'd think about coming back, but he's like those old men who've never thrown away a *Life* magazine or a piece of string. With him it's mostly medical journals. He's not thrown one away since he'd been in medical school, nor any books either. Lots of other junk around, too, parts of old motors, rusty tools. . . . Two dead cars are in the garage. He has to park his diesel sedan in the driveway.

When the doctor and his third wife bought this house, the wife kept things more or less cleaned up. If she was still with him things wouldn't have gotten quite so out of hand. She never did like having all this stuff, but it was in some control and mostly out of sight. Actually the house was full of junk from the moment they moved in.

The doctor loves a big house like this. When his wife was still with him they could invite guests to stay over. He likes to play the paterfamilias. Of course he can't do that anymore. Now he does it in a smaller way. Whenever he goes to a party he always brings big chunks of cheeses and special black bread. Sometimes a ham. Sometimes a five pound bag of pistachios. Always more food than anybody can use in a week.

His dog died shortly after his wife left him. He buried it in the back yard. That dog. . . . Twelve years before he had taken home a sick, mangy puppy, slept with it on his chest and got mange himself. It was a type of mange that human beings are not supposed to get. The puppy grew up to be the dog that died.

But on the other hand, the doctor taught heart surgery by having the students operate on dogs.

The house badly needs painting, but the doctor doesn't notice. If he did, and though it's a huge job, he'd probably plan to paint it himself. He'd buy the paint and keep it in the garage or the basement and now and then think about doing it.

The cats started more recently when the doctor discovered a family of feral cats in his garage and began feeding them. One was pregnant. It was getting colder so the doctor made a little cat door into his basement. It gave them the run of the house.

He's not sure how many cats are in there now. And he thinks he saw a possum.

The cats are mostly tabbies, some gingers, a calico or two. . . . Only one is white. That's his favorite. White cats always have a hard time hunting. They're so easily seen. And she's smaller. She's the underdog cat. He has always loved underdogs best. Besides, she's so luminous. She seems to glow in the dark. He named her Nimbus. He wonders about her fur. He looked at it under the microscope to see if he could see what caused the sheen. Too bad he doesn't have a normal white cat to compare it with, but wild white cats don't last long. He wonders how this one survived to grow up.

They're all still pretty wild. They won't let him pick them up. So far only two sit on his lap. They're nocturnal and the doctor's not home in the daytime to keep them awake. There's a lot of action through the night. They've staked out their territory and defend it with caterwauling. The doctor has learned to sleep through it.

He leaves paper grocery bags on the floors all around the house because the cats like to go into them. Also cardboard boxes here and there.

Even though he can't pick any of them up, if he sits quietly (and he makes a point of sitting quietly) one might jump into his lap.

He doesn't go on vacation anymore because he can't leave the animals. He doesn't attend medical conferences. Even going away for a weekend might be dangerous for them. Nobody could ever be persuaded to come in there to feed them. He wonders what they would do if something happened to him.

The minute he comes in, he says Hello to all the cats in the kitchen. (Some of them are good at meowing back to him.) He comes in the back door, the front door is never used and wasn't even when his wife was here. There's a nice little porch out front but it's never been used either.

The doctor brings in forsythia and pussy willows to force into bloom. On hands and knees, he puts in tulip bulbs, thinking all the time that, instead, (if, that is, he had actually noticed the need for paint and bought it) he should be painting the house or at least starting to. He has no illusions about what a big job it is and how long it'll take but he thinks himself capable of anything regardless of his age.

The doctor brings in a large cocoon. It was hanging on a limb right over where he parks his car. He's surprised he didn't notice it before since that's exactly the kind of thing he always notices. He brings in the whole branch and nails it on the wall over the breakfast nook. High enough so the cats can't get to it.

What is born in the warmth of the kitchen is a moth of unusual beauty. The doctor can't bring himself to put it in alcohol, pin it and put it up on his wall along with the others in his collection, even though it's the largest and most beautiful of any of them.

The moth won't survive these cats. He takes it upstairs and puts it in the master bedroom where there's a big bay window. (He doesn't sleep there anymore.) He shoos out the cats and shuts the door. Of course it won't last long. It doesn't have a mouth. It's purely a sex creature, alive, not to eat, but to copulate.

Fairy dust covers his hands.

The third wife never comes around to the house. It pains her to look at it. He won't let anybody in anyway. They always meet someplace else—at a nice restaurant or at a movie. Last date they had, the third wife thought the doctor looked a little odd, kind of fuzzy . . . greenish, mossy. . . .

And he smells odd. Not so much the damp man-smell of sweat, though that, too, but musky and marshy—a smell of growing things. It's sexy but it worries her.

The house itself is sending out waves of pheromones that bring yet more creatures to the little cat door into the basement. Nobody can guess what's in there now.

Finally the smells bring the third wife.

It's so dim in there and there's this odd strong smell. She's not sure if a good smell or bad one. At first it makes her choke. She goes back out but then she sees eyes . . . two huge scary black eyes peering out at her from an upper window. What might be up there looking out with such big eyes? Maybe the smell is the smell of death. (Unlike the doctor, the third wife doesn't know what death smells like.)

The third wife puts her hand over her nose and mouth and goes back into the kitchen, moving slowly. It's hot outside, but not bad in the house. It's three stories high, and it's shaded by big trees, and the doctor has pulled all the shades to keep it cool.

At first she sees shiny eyes all around her and there's scuffling noises. She steps around boxes and stacks of magazines. She steps on a paper bag. Something yowls and tears out of it in a fury.

Then she sees Nimbus on a high kitchen shelf. The doctor has already told the third wife about her—how he looked at her fur under the microscope—how it had a glassy quality.

The third wife is wearing white. She's almost as luminous as Nimbus. One wonders how long she can be in here and keep her skirt and blouse clean.

She calls out, Are you there? It's me. It's me. Calls out, Honey? Dear?

One wonders who, or how many, out of all these creatures, might answer.

Does she dare go on, farther in? Is the doctor even

home? But what about those strange big eyes in the upstairs window? The Doctor might be up there helpless, at the mercy of. . . . Or sick . . . maybe sick from his own house-smells.

She heads up the narrow back stairs that go straight from the kitchen. She wonders: Is he still sleeping where he used to sleep? There are two big bedrooms, a big bed in each. He might be in either. Though what if those rooms have gotten filled up with junk? He might have had to move to a smaller one.

Then she thinks maybe she should have called the hospital first, to see if he was there. You never know when he might be operating. He's called out at all hours. (She always thought it odd that he never seemed to mind. She remembers one Christmas dinner, all the family there, the turkey just brought out. . . .) But she's come too far now, she might as well take a look.

The upstairs hallway is narrow and dark by the back stairs but broadens out for the fancier bedrooms. It's daytime, but it's awfully dim back in the narrow part of the hall. Cats have followed her. The white cat, in its catty way, circling her feet, first one side and then the other. She has to be careful not to step on her.

At the far end, where the hall broadens out, there's a window with a dirty lace curtain. The window sends out dusty beams of light. The third wife can see . . . or she thinks she sees, tiny creatures in the dust, flying in the light. But how would you know the difference, dust or bugs?

But where *is* the doctor? She calls, "Honey? Are you there?"

She'll go on. She has to see if the doctor is all right.

The white cat still circles her legs, purring now.

"Honey?"

She was right about the first big bedroom. Nobody could sleep in there. There isn't room. The shades are drawn against the heat and the third wife sees the gleam of a few sets of eyes. She backs out and shuts the door.

It's from the window of the second big room that she had seen the huge eyes staring at her while she was still outside. She doesn't want to look in there, she's scared to, but it might be important.

As she opens the door, something flutters out from behind the curtain. That's what the eyes were. Big wings with huge eyes on them. And it seems as if it's looking at her but of course that can't be. Those eyes are phony—meant only to scare, but they work. She can't help but step back and huddle into herself.

The big, big-eyed moth follows her out of the room and back down the hall, always just a few yards behind. It seems to be growing. The third wife wonders if that's really happening or if she's just scared. And she wonders if it's true about moths not having mouths. Maybe *some* do.

She finally gets to the little maid's room. As she opens the door somebody says, "Come in. I've been waiting for you. Waiting and waiting." The voice is deep, resonant. Growly. Is it really her husband's? Perhaps he's sick. He sounds sick. But it's a voice full of love. The third wife wonders how she ever could have brought herself to leave him.

The white cat goes in first. She lights the room with her glow. But the third wife's white blouse glows, too. The moth comes in last. The third wife thinks it's grown to the size of a blanket.

There's something long, lumpy, and greenish lying on the maid's little bed.

The wife lies down beside . . . it . . . him . . . whatever it is that's so warm and soft . . . that smells both very good and very bad. Lies down and sinks in. First she thinks, I'm sorry I came and right after that, I'm glad I came.

She says it, "I'm glad I came," and, "I'm glad you're all right."

The thing beside her growls. She always thought he was sort of like a bear.

The neighbors across the street don't call the fire engines. They don't mind such a ramshackle eyesore burning down—good riddance, though too bad about the oak paneling and the oak staircase. And there are too many cats. Besides, they know the doctor is almost always at the hospital so there's nobody there to be rescued. They had been glad the deer preferred the doctor's yard to their own—glad possums and raccoons stayed over there. Even the crows like the doctor's land best.

Up from the flames comes a big black cloud and out from it, sparkling ashes rain down.

Everybody in the little town nearby wakes up and looks out the window. They think somebody has set off firecrackers. They haven't seen such a good show in a long time.

BOUNTIFUL CITY

WALKING AROUND SAYING, I love you, I love you, I love you, and not being in love with anybody . . . . Perhaps it's too much coffee. Or the air today, transparent—pinkish. It usually isn't. After all, it's the city, everything black and gray. Chewing gum stuck all over the sidewalk. And spit. A quarter falls and you hate to pick it up. You get soot in your eye. But that won't happen today.

I love. I love. I could fall in love with the very next man who appears. I check them all out. Compare mustaches. Lots these days. How nice to smooth one. Or stroke a beard. Stroke rough man cheeks. Chest hair. Small of the back hair.

The city glimmers. I'm looking at the tops of buildings, not down at the spit. All kinds of architecture all mixed up, up there. Some shine golden. Some painted Aztec colors: aqua and dull peach. Some art nouveau.

But how nice, right this minute, to be bouncing along the street looking up, but also into faces. Smiling. Evaluating. Thinking about beards and eyebrows. Thinking, I love you, I love you, but who? Love. How nice to be in it.

Except for the yearning. That's the hard part.

Where *is* somebody?

My goal in life is this one thing. (As if it hasn't always been.)

Walk proudly. But not too proud. You never know what the man in question might like best in his women. I won't be anything particular until I find out his taste.

There goes a possible man right now. I always did like skinny dark ones. And here's another right behind him. What a generous world!

The look in the eye is important. I peer. I stare. Here's another one. He's wearing a cowboy hat (I was always a sucker for a big hat). He's not from around here. What wonderfully bushy eyebrows! He's from out West. Patience is needed with animals especially horses. A patient man would be nice. Of course patience is needed in the city, too. Just crossing the street can be aggravating. And all that honking.

I wonder if he's rich. Of course he could be a farmer, not an oil man.

Even so I turn and follow that one. I don't remember if he had a kind eye. His mustache was so big I didn't notice anything else.

But I don't want any short-term relationships, I want somebody from right here. I turn back. I wander on with all the other walkers. I watch the Chrysler building roof glimmer in the setting sun.

Here's another man. Hat, dark suit, black turtleneck makes him look all the thinner. I turn and follow him. His legs are nice and straight, not like some.

How begin? Drop my package? Trip him?

When's the proper time to say, I love you? How long do I have to wait? I've been saying it to myself at every step. I may not be able to hold myself back. I put a cough drop in my mouth to keep me quiet, and follow.

Besides, love can go bad. Love can turn with the weather. I'll not commit myself until I'm sure.

(I have a picture in my purse of a man I never met. I cut it out of a magazine. Perhaps now's the time to throw it out—before some other man sees it and thinks things.

Though I hate to. What if no other man ever works out? At least I'll have this one.)

New Yorkers walk for miles. It's the most walking city in the world, I'll bet. Now four of us: a trench coat guy, a girl with upscale backpack, my man, me. . . . We've gone on for an hour as though we knew each other. From West 57th to East 15th. That's the way it always is in New York. The girl and I have smiled at each other though none of the men have. The girl turns off on 14th but the rest of us keep going, down, down, downtown. It's getting late and I'm hungry.

I almost lose him as he turns on 4th, stops for a newspaper. I do, too. I look deep into his eyes. I put all my yearning in that one glance. You'd think he'd notice but he doesn't. Or perhaps he's afraid of commitment. I know his kind.

He's up the steps and in his building—not a very nice one—before I have a chance to trip him or drop my package. I had hoped he'd let me in. I could have said I was delivering my package. (I've bought new shoes. I was happy with them. That's another reason I was feeling so full of love.)

Where will I go from here? Walk all the way back up to Central Park?

But a light goes on in a basement apartment right beside the front door. I hunker down and look in and there he is, taking off his jacket. What a room! He needs a wife, that's for sure. Well now I know a bit about who he is. I'd feel claustrophobic in there.

Two other black turtlenecks exactly like the one he's wearing are on the bed. Silky black socks all over the place. Piles of books and papers sideways on the floor because of no bookcases. No plants. I could see to that, though there's no place for them. If I cleaned it up, there might be room for a little stand by the window.

There's a pile of ropes in a corner on the floor. A funny pair of shoes on top. They're kind of like ballet slippers but with more rubber. What's the meaning of those?

I keep squatting down, watching. He cooks himself a couple of eggs on his hot plate. Sits on his bed to eat. He doesn't have a table. His bottle of wine is on the floor. He drinks straight out of the bottle.

After eating, he takes off his turtleneck. I evaluate his chest. He's got muscles and nice curly black hair in the middle.

He flops on the bed, which is smaller than a twin bed. How could we make love on that? Besides, it's sagging. Maybe we should do it on the floor instead.

Then he realizes he hasn't pulled his curtains. He gets up, comes and looks right at me. Stares. Jerks the curtains shut.

I'll go home and write some love poems.

Next morning, early, I go down there first thing and squat by his window. The curtains are open and he's gone.

I go up to the cloisters. I imagine he might be there. I glance around every corner, hoping . . . yearning. . . . Then I walk through Central Park. I sit on a bench and wait but nobody like him comes along.

I wander Lincoln Center for an hour. I go to the Museum of Modern Art. I eat lunch there. I sit with a notebook and pretend to write love poems. I don't keep my nose in it. I look around. I stare into space a lot. If I was really writing a love poem that's what I'd be doing, anyway, waiting for inspiration. I see several possibilities . . . almost good enough, but he doesn't come.

If I ever do see him again, will he recognize me as the one who looked in his window? He did stare at me—a long stare.

I go up to the top of the Empire State Building. Same waiting. Same looking around the deck. There's somebody there who's almost right. Still, I like my man best.

I stay up there a whole hour. Yearning out in every direction.

Then I hear sirens. I look over the side and I see police cars and fire engines down below. Crowds gathering. And here's a helicopter hovering right across from me. All of a sudden the roof is full of cops and firemen. Several look interesting. Lots of mustaches. Some sideburns.

Even as I look over the side to see what's up, I strike a pose, one knee cocked, toe pointed. Since I'm wearing running shoes, I know the effect won't be exactly what I hope.

My god, somebody is climbing the Empire State Building. He looks like a fly down there. There's nothing to hold him up but his fingers. How can anybody do that?

The cops are going to arrest him the minute he gets up here. They're calm, guns and handcuffs ready.

He's going slowly. Well, fast for what he's doing, I suppose. I'm holding my breath. I didn't realize it until I started feeling woozy. I take long slow breaths, counting four beats to each. It looks like the cop standing next to me has to do the same.

The man climbs closer. Black turtleneck, black pants. He looks up and it's him. *My* man. We're two of a kind. Him and his love of climbing and me with my just plain love or love of love. I'm all in black, too. It's not only the New York color, it's slimming and mysterious and sexy.

How nice that there are two sexes. Everywhere one looks one finds one or the other, and especially how nice that there's the other. Bulges one place or another. (In some languages even the chairs and tables have a sex.) The whole world as if for me. Like this policeman right beside me. I match my breathing with his so as to be sure not to forget that I have to breathe.

Look at those black eyes as my man looks up. At me. Surely he knows I'm the one who walked from West 57th Street to East 4th Street with him. Surely he remembers closing his curtains when he saw me looking in.

I'm so proud. Who else could do this besides my man? I feel even more love than I already did. I can't wait till he gets up here.

But can he climb over and around that net they have in place to keep people from jumping? Not from jumping, but from landing on the sidewalk. Of course he can.

What should I do when he gets here? Should I try to keep the police from arresting him? Should I distract them?

The roof is full of people now. A lot of newspeople, too. I'm glad I came up hours ago to wait and watch for him. I have the perfect spot. People try to push me aside, but I have a good grip on the railing.

Here he comes. I knew it, the net is no problem for somebody like him.

I start yelling and pretend to be about to jump over the edge to greet him. The policemen grab me. I wave my arms and slap at them. I want my man to see how I'm fighting for him.

Now the cameras are turned on me instead of him. There's much more action where I am than where he is. I put on a good show.

They arrest him and haul him off. I wonder where? Perhaps he'll be home on 4th Street after posting bail.

As soon as he's gone from the platform, I calm down—on purpose. I become completely reasonable. I don't get arrested. I talk them out of it. I say that was my lover and I went a little bit crazy until he got safely up here. They understand. I go down the elevator with them. They're almost all attractive. They glow with man sweat. Many need a shave. I'd kiss their cheeks if I dared. I think of their hairy bodies. New York's finest. Is that what they say? They hardly notice me. They talk man talk . . . swearing in their deep, scratchy voices. I could fall in love with the voice alone. The deepest voice comes from a skinny little man hardly taller than I am. I'm thinking of changing my love over to him, but climbing a building is more romantic than a deep voice . . . unless he sings. I've always loved basses. How can he be a policeman and be so small? I suppose he knows karate or some such. And he has such thick glasses. I'll stick to my climber. Though I've never heard him sing. I haven't even heard him speak.

Maybe he'll love me if. . . . Well *if* a lot of things: I learn to cook, or learn to sing. Dance. I could get fatter, or maybe thinner. I *might* have the courage to climb buildings beside him, both of us in danger together. That might fuel our love.

How be my best self in front of him? Or better than I really am? Show my giving side.

I'll use all the words. In succession. I'll say, "Beloved." "Knowing you . . . or rather having seen you, I've become aware of things I've never been aware of before. The air, the flowers, (after all it's spring), the stars. . . ." (Hard to see any stars in the city. Hardly ever notice the moon. But now I seek it out from behind the street lights. And it's there.)

Oh how I want to hurry through the preliminaries and be as if we'd known each other months. Forget the getting acquainted. Jump right into the middle. On the bed. In his case on the mattress on the floor, the bed not being suitable for two.

Love should never go to waste no matter if a person is fat or thin or has a long nose or pigeon-toes.

But it's spring. A time to revel. Revel in tulips coming up in the little plots of dirt around the trees. Revel in my innocence. Because when have I ever made love before? It's certainly been years. (Does one keep one's innocence if one reads all about it? Sees it in the movies? That Japanese one, for instance, where she puts a chicken's egg up herself and then lays it? Would that be something he'd like?)

Spring, the perfect season for innocence. Crocuses especially. All I've known of sex is already forgotten.

I get so excited I trot down to 4th Street to see if he's home yet.

He's not, but I sneak in with an old lady who holds the door for me though she's never seen me before. There's a nice spot under the stairs. I hunker down with the snow shovel and the broom and mop. It's been such a long exciting day I fall asleep right away.

Well not quite. I think about him. Wonder what he

does when he's not climbing the Empire State Building? How does he make money? Cat burglar? Climb straight up brick walls? I won't turn him in. I'll stick by him no matter what.

But isn't he tempting fate by all this publicity? How will it help his cat burglar career to be in all the papers.

And *then* I fall asleep.

I miss him coming home. It's six a.m. when I knock on his door. I keep knocking until I hear a growl. Then he says, Go away, without even knowing who it is.

"It's me." I whisper it. "Me. Me."

Is now the time to say, I love you?

"I'm the one at the top of the Empire State Building. I waited for you all day and you came."

Not the time to say I love you.

(Even to love is embarrassing. How odd that it should be so.)

But nothing ventured nothing gained.

"I love you."

"Who are you?"

How answer such a question? I'm ready to be anything he wants.

"I am your hearts desire. If not that right now, I'm willing to learn."

"Go away. It's six a.m."

"I'll wait."

I sit down with my back against the door.

I hear him getting up, taking a shower, listening to the news. It's the very same station I always listen to.

By now it's eight o'clock.

He unlocks three locks including the police lock (I can hear its clank), opens the door, sees me, and slams it shut again. I hear the police lock thump into place. Who does he think I am, anyway? I couldn't even get in a normal lock.

"Go away. I'm not coming out until you leave."

I could say I'll leave and then not do it, but then he'd think I wasn't a very nice person.

"I'll leave. I'm leaving right now. I'm doing exactly

what you tell me to and I always will. Goodbye."

First thing, outside, I buy a newspaper, and there we both are! There's one picture of him climbing up and another of me waving my arms and with my mouth open, yelling. I don't look very attractive that way. I must make sure not to do that again.

I stop at a cappuccino shop and read the article. People protested his arrest. They got together and raised his bail and the cops let him go. I don't come off too well. They call me a hysterical woman, claiming to be . . . "claiming," they said . . . his girlfriend.

I walk back to my place, thinking, I love you, I love you, at every step. Thousands of steps and thousands of I love yous. I just love. I don't care. It can be anybody. But even if I were to be in love with somebody else, I'm not going to let him get away with the way he's been behaving. I won't be ignored—as if I'm nobody. I may actually *be* nobody, but he shouldn't rub it in. He shouldn't just jump to that conclusion before he even knows who I am. Besides, after the newspaper article, I'm not nobody anymore. Though, actually, I don't think anybody will recognize me from that picture with my mouth stretched out so far. They won't know I'm somebody now—as of yesterday. I didn't give them my right name and address. I was afraid to. So I'm still not somebody.

At least I know *his* name—from the newspapers. He already was somebody. The Great Buzzoni. Not a cat burglar after all. A high wire artist. I don't know how he makes his living doing that. Especially living here in New York. Though he does have a cheap apartment. Maybe he's *also* a cat burglar.

Next day I stake myself out near his apartment. With a purse full of diet bars. I wear a big hat. I hope men like women in big hats as much as I like men in them. Lots of front steps across from his place to sit on while I wait.

Finally here he comes, a beret instead of a hat this time. A neat quick man. No wonder I followed him.

I've figured out what to say. I say it. "Hello. It's me. I

saw you climbing."

He walks right by. In fact he walks even faster. I have a hard time keeping up.

I shout after him, "I climb, too. I'd like to climb with you. Both of us climbing would be even more of a show. The Great Gabriella. And when I said, I love you, I meant I love the way you climb."

I wonder if I can do it. I've always been afraid of heights. I'll have to find a brick building to try it on. I'll practice in an alley so nobody will see.

Now he's slowing down. Now he turns around. He looks at me—really looks. "You can?"

We walk to the corner for coffee. I can't believe I'm walking beside the great Buzzoni and that I picked him out on the street, from millions of people. I forgive him for telling me to go away that morning.

(For all his sharp Italian looks, his name is really George Mayer. I wonder what I should say my real name is.)

We don't talk about climbing. And I don't dare ask how he makes his living. He doesn't ask me either. I suppose for the same reason. We might both be cat burglars. If he's one, all the more reason to think I'm one. We ask each other everything but that.

(I'm glad I ordered the same things he did. It makes us more companionable.)

We're nature lovers, though here in New York there's not much nature to love: Cockroaches, rats, and pigeons, but it's spring. Some sort of sparrows are chirping in the trees.

We're lovers of beauty, sunsets and sunrises, and here he is living in a basement. Out his window he can watch feet. I have a better view from my fifth floor walk up.

What if he needs a helper? Dare I ask?

I ask.

He sits and thinks.

"All right. I could use somebody."

I still don't know what for.

"Tuesday, two weeks from now. Midnight. 17th Street at Broadway."

Good, that gives me time to practice.

He walks me partway home just for my company. He shakes my hand when he leaves and I feel his strong calloused fingers. Shaking mine does he know? He must.

"I'm a little out of practice."

His are not lover's hands. I wouldn't want them on my body. How will we manage love without his hands?

Luckily my own window looks out on a back alley so that's where I try to get up to, but even if I lived on the second floor, I'd not make it. I get up about a foot and hang there until my fingers give out. With him by my side I'm sure I can do more, but not much.

I practice all those two weeks, but I don't get much better. Maybe a little stronger. Mostly I ruin my fingers. Once I make it all the way up to five feet. Next day I lapse back to three. I fall a lot.

I know myself. I may have acrophobia but I can steel myself against it. For his sake, anyway. When you feel your stomach turning upside down just look out at the horizon—if you can see any such thing from in the city.

Down is harder.

What if I get up several floors and get stuck there all alone?

Finally I get far enough up to sneak into somebody's second floor window. It's the middle of the day. Everybody's at work. Nobody sees me. I should steal something so I'll be of a kind with him—in danger of being arrested. Our philosophy of life will be the same. I don't know what to take. I look around. Lots of books and papers and not much else. I open all the drawers. No jewelry. None at all. Looks as if somebody has already stolen everything worth taking. Maybe he did it. What's left for me to take? A book? A potted plant? That doesn't seem like much.

I lie down on the bed to think about it and fall asleep by

mistake. When I wake up it's getting dark. I've got to leave fast. I grab the clock beside the bed and run out the door. Just in time because people are coming in downstairs.

I wish I'd taken clothes. I could use a new blouse. I already have a clock almost exactly like this one.

I do feel a sense of accomplishment, though. And I feel closer to him now I know what it's like to do as he does.

I love, I love. . . . What a world, so full of beards and lips! So soft. In fact all sorts of soft things. Velvety things.

I've been so busy practicing I haven't gone down to his place at all, but then the time comes for our meeting.

(I'm wearing black tights and black turtleneck top. Climbing clothes. I look slim and romantic.)

The city at night! Like a Christmas tree no matter the season. And how nice to be walking beside him, matching his stride.

But maybe he's not a cat burglar after all. Turns out he needs someone to help find a spot between two skyscrapers where he can set up a tightrope—in the middle of the night so nobody will know. He needs somebody to help set it up. He wants to use the flatiron building if possible. It's always windy around there so it'll be dangerous but he likes that all the better.

We check it out. It's not possible. We walk up town to search for other places. Perhaps Lincoln Center. Not high up but long.

When we stop for coffee I say first thing, "I thought you were a cat burglar." He looks startled—as if I'd found him out. Or maybe just that he hadn't ever thought of doing that before.

"Oh, I don't mind. I do it myself."

He's still looking shocked. Even more so.

"I don't ever take valuable things."

Have I made myself unlovable in just one sentence?

"I only take little things. Actually I've only taken one thing . . . ever."

I don't like the way he's looking at me.

"Actually I've never climbed beyond the second floor."

Why doesn't he say something?

"Actually I only did it for you. And I brought you this."

I try to give him the clock. (He already has one exactly like it, too. I saw it in his apartment.)

He waves it away.

He hasn't said a word since I mentioned cat burglar.

Do I know his secret?

You should never know a man's secret, especially if it's illegal—though I'm part of that now myself.

Well, that's the end of that. I can see it in his eyes. Even with the gift.

There's plenty more—men that is. Maybe I should forget about them altogether. But I don't want to.

"I can get you more things."

I guess not.

We part. Not even with a kiss.

Anyway, his eyes were too close together, he's too short, I'm just as tall as he is. His voice is the opposite of bass.

The moon is out. The city shines. It's full of men. I look into faces. I stare. I check out ways of walking. I follow first one and then another. Bald men with hairy bodies. Hairy men with smooth bodies. Joe, Pete, Sam, Henry, Louis, Bob, Charley. . . .

COO PEOPLE

W E'VE LIVED HIDDEN in your cities for longer than we
can remember. Top floors, mostly. Word of mouth
. . . *our* word of mouth, tells us we've been here since your
cities began. How we've managed is, we pretend we're
you, dress like you, wear your kinds of hairdos, when
your eyeglasses have little wings at the sides, ours do,
too. We walk around looking at things that you'd look at,
otherwise we'd be staring at your ceilings all the time. We
thumb through your *Playboy* and *Cosmopolitan* whether
we like them or not, we get the *TV Guide* and watch what
you watch so we can talk about it with you, we jump and
yell as much as you do at your baseball games, we read
your best sellers, look at your art shows. It's all pretend.
We've forgotten our own kind of art. We don't even dare
think about it. We may have lost our art forever though
it's better than yours. Or so we always tell each other.
We used to have our own language, too. We say it was so
full of asides and embellishments that it was of a beauty
inconceivable to anyone but us.

Even your doctors can't tell we're us. Of course they
wouldn't suspect anyway since they don't know we exist.

If you knew about us, we don't know what you'd do.
You've never liked the different. Especially you don't like

those people who are fairly close to exactly what you are yourselves. So—dull and drab . . . invisible is what we aspire to. How else live among you and get along as well as we do?

We only trust each other. We only dare tell each other about ourselves when we're old enough to handle the information. That's about ten years old. To us, all the wonderful things about ourselves are more interesting than sex. Unimportant, some would say, but wonderful anyway. "Dear Child, you're entirely different from everybody else except us and you were born to dance."

Most of the time we know who we are. There's our springy walk, our singsong voices, our screechy laugh. And we're double-jointed. If you can't bend your thumb down to touch your forearm, you're not one of us. (Even if you *can* do it, you may not be one of us, anyway.) And, though just a teeny tiny bit, we can fly. I shouldn't call it flying. It's more like lift. We can lift a little bit and if frightened or exhilarated we can, *maybe*, make it over a car—a small one. There's not much need for such a talent. It's hardly worth having. And when your life depends on never being noticed, it's a big bother because when we get excited, sometimes we have to hold each other down. And *always* we have to hold down our babies. Until they get their balance that is. By the time they can sit up, they can usually keep themselves down except when they're too happy. We sew little weights into their clothing. Otherwise you'd know that we were us. We take the weights out when the child has more control, though with some children. . . .

We came to the cities in the first place—or so we always tell each other . . . (Oral history is all we have. It's too dangerous to write things down) . . . came because we wanted your city advantages: opera and ballet. *Especially* ballet. That little bit of lift makes us good dancers, though we have to make sure not to overdo it.

I'm just in the corps de ballet. It's never good for us to be soloists.

Nijinsky was one of us. He went mad because of having

to keep himself secret without any time off. He should have had a vacation from dancing now and then, before it was too late, and gone back to one of our secret retreats to rest up from always being surrounded by *you* people. We need to go away every once in a while or we'll go crazy just as Nijinsky did.

I can't think what use that little bit of lift could be except as a help in ballet. (Though it's also good for magicians lifting beautiful women with no visible means of support. In our case there actually is no means of support.) As far as I know, it's just a bother trying to hide it and trying not to do it when we're excited and happy. It's always safer for us to be sad.

But now I go coo, coo, cooing as if a mourning dove. I try to stop, because who else but one of us would do such a thing? But I'm too happy. If I didn't coo I'd lift by mistake. I sing, coo, as if a song of spring even though we've already had the first snow. You don't look as crazy if you coo in springtime. I hope people do think I'm crazy so as not to think I might be one of us, and then go on to realize that we exist.

(I think we coo because our mouths like the shape of it.)

But oh, coooo, I've met a man. Unfortunately he's one of you. He doesn't look like us. He's dark and broad and muscled. I can't imagine him having any lift at all.

He has a broken nose. I like it. He also has a bald head with a fringe of black hair around the edges. I like that, too.

First thing this man said to me was, "I know who *you* are."

I got scared. I thought he meant he knew about *us*, but he just meant he knew my name. I don't know how. Perhaps he's been to the ballet, though he doesn't seem the type.

We talked for a minute. He just moved in to my building. He lives on the first floor. We couldn't stand living that far down. I felt so good that he'd stopped to talk to me, I heard very little of what he said. I just looked into those glittery black eyes. I wish I'd listened. I wonder what it was he was telling me.

I know a few things about him from listening to people in the lobby. He's a fireman, so he does all sorts of things it would be better for *us* to be doing considering they often involve heights, but we're not strong enough for that. We have a lot of endurance, but we're willowy. They say he loves the risks but we can't take any in case we reveal ourselves. They don't think he rescues because he cares about people, he just wants to take another risk. He likes storms and fires and earthquakes—all sorts of catastrophes. And he rescues even when he's on vacation. He just can't stop. It's his passion.

We must, as is easy to see, only mate with our own kind, otherwise we might lose our double joints and our only talent. Whatever children *this* man might have would be the opposite of us: wild and free and into everything and much too big.

I've tried not to fall in love with your kind, and, up until a few days ago, it was easy not to, even though there are many men among you that could be said to be my type; but I never cared anything about them.

Right after I first met him, I saw him at our apartment roof party. He didn't dance, but he was swaying a little bit. You'd not think a man of his nature would sway. We looked at each other. He might have winked. (He doesn't seem the type to wink either.) Perhaps he was looking at somebody behind me. I looked to see who was there, but even though she was beautiful, I'm not sure which of us he was looking at. I'm not so bad looking myself—if you like your blond hair lank.

I sneaked up behind him and eavesdropped. I heard him tell yet another beautiful girl that he was going off to the mountains, to Manchester Peak to join their search and rescue team for a vacation. I'll go to that mountain, too. I'm going to see if he'll rescue me. Of course he might be out rescuing somebody else at the time I'm in trouble, but I'll take that chance. He doesn't like the city. I suppose he stays because of all the fires and rescues, though of course there's plenty of rescuing to be done in the mountains. Maybe he doesn't like rescuing out there because those mountain accidents are so often from carelessness or stupidity. (Exactly what I'm going to be: stupid.)

So I'm off to climb Manchester Peak where that man is vacationing. I mean I'll *start* to. I hope I don't have to go too far. I hope a snowstorm comes. I'll listen to the weather report and if it says not to go I'll go.

Since it's fall, it's a risky stupid season for going as high as I plan to go, but it has to be a real rescue. He'd know if it was phony. Up in that altitude I suppose I'll be able to lift all the more. Or will it be the opposite because the air is thinner?

I hope I don't inadvertently skim over snow drifts to make things easy for myself after I've sunk in up to my crotch. I hope I remember (even when I get tired) to at least have my toes dragging in the snow so I look right in case somebody sees.

I have to get the paraphernalia for it. Carabiners, ropes, pitons, ax, and such. A lot to carry but I have to look as if I'm making a serious (if stupid) try. (I doubt if I can lift with all this stuff, but I can drop a lot of those things along the way so as to leave a good trail.)

Of course I might get rescued by some entirely different person. Most likely some old hermit who lives in the mountains all year long in a smelly hovel and never says a word to anybody. There are still a few of those people around.

I wonder if it would be a good thing to sprain my ankle? And when would be the best time for it, early on or farther up? (We never sprain our ankles. Our lifting is a reflex. Hard not to do it when we're about to fall down. I wouldn't know how, but I suppose I could figure out some way—slip my foot between two rocks and then. . . . I don't even want to think about it.)

So here I am exactly where I want to be, out in the middle of nowhere cooing in a whisper, one coo to each breath, and looking up at the snowy tops of things: snowy trees, snowy mountains. . . . We like white best of all. It's so airy. Of course we like blue, too. It's so sky.

I begin dropping things right away, carabiners first. After those the pitons. (I hope the snow doesn't cover everything up.) Then I let go the ax. I may be sorry but, if I drop such an important thing, that's a sure sign I'm in trouble. Leaving that takes as much courage as spraining my ankle would, but I laugh out loud anyway because of where I am and what's (maybe) going to happen.

It isn't until I'm stuck, having slipped . . . *let* myself slip (*we* don't slip) onto an icy ledge and can't go up or down, *nor* sideways (exactly what I wanted to have happen) that I think: What if he watches me even right this very minute to see, now that I'm in real trouble, what I'm going to do next? I can't wait to see what I'll do next myself. Actually I don't do anything. I wait.

But. . . . Oh for Heaven's sake! Here's one of those wizened old, hermit kind of men I was thinking about before. He's above me, leaning towards me with an unraveling old rope, unraveling black knit cap, unraveling black sweater, whiskey voice that hardly sounds out. I can't hear him. I have to guess what he's saying. It's most likely, "Grab the rope."

I almost tell him to go away. I'll not let anyone come between me and what's supposed to happen. But I think twice and I do grab the rope. At least I won't have to test how I lift in this altitude. I won't have to find out whether, if I jump off a cliff this high, I'll be able to land softly.

At the top I reach and grab his hands—or rather his unraveling mittens. I stare at him. He's a willowy man. I'm wondering if he's one of us. I'm wondering if he's wondering if I'm one of us, too.

I see he has my carabiners hanging all over him, and, at his belt, clipped on by one of my carabiners, he's got my brand new ax.

The mind's eye sees more clearly than the eye. The mind's eye ought to trust itself. Understanding comes later—*usually* does, and always in the middle of the night.

And it *is* the middle of the night, though so far I've not understood anything. I'm bedded down in an alcove, covered with half a dozen old army blankets, listening to the old man snore. This is probably where he sleeps but he's on the floor across the room by the dry sink.

He only has this one room and it's full of art—if you can call this art. I don't know what art is any more than I know who I and we are, but the room is full of complicated things with curlicues and convolutions, twists and whorls. You can hardly tell where one begins and another ends. Or maybe they are all just one sculpture. There's hardly room to walk around. It's not like your art at all. It's stormy looking and lumpy. . . . There's a hint of wings. (Hermes was one of us, wings on his feet where they ought to be.)

The old man told me this is how he spends the time when it storms. I asked him, but how did he happen to be out so as to rescue me?

"I fear my dog has met with coyotes and either been killed by them or run off with them. Most likely killed. I was looking for him."

He has a funny accent. I can't place it. He actually rolls his r's and he asked me if I'd "et." You don't suppose. . . . Could it be that that's from speaking our old lost language?

I wish I knew more about what our art used to be like. Who would dare carve things like this but way out in the woods? (Hack out is a better way to say it.) There's nothing shocking to it as to sex, but it looks shocking anyway. Maybe there is sexuality to it and I just don't know enough to see it. Or maybe it's the power of it that shocks me. Or maybe just that it's so different.

Nothing is worse than different. We're all taught that first thing. All of you are also taught that, too. And nothing is more the same than ballet. Full of rules of how it used to be done so we can do it exactly that way now. Even our bows are choreographed according to how they used to do it. It's said, "Good ballet is never blunted by verisimilitude." There's no verisimilitude to blunt this man's art either.

But I don't want to think about it. I turn away and try to sleep though all these sculptured things looming over me are scary.

And I *do* have a midnight revelation. I wake up suddenly when I finally realize that that fireman probably isn't in search of me at all, but of *us!* All of us, maybe including this old man? Maybe he's been sent out by the government? I can't let him hear this old man's accent. I can't let him see this . . . art.

Even so, perhaps when he winked, it really *was* for me.

In the morning I look out the door first thing—at the sun and the shiny snow—and see somebody wearing camouflage. A broad man, looking at the shack through field glasses.

I start to coo again. I can't help it. The old man gives me a look I can't read. Well, we hardly ever talk about being us unless we're at one of our retreats and even then we don't talk much about it. We just give each other raised eyebrows and such. I stop my cooing right away and switch to an entrechat starting from fifth position. I *have* to do something. If he's us he'll know I'm us, too, and if he's not us, he'll think I'm crazy.

Then I see the dog, limping up to that camouflaged man. You can't fool a dog no matter how much you look like a tree in fall foliage. Besides, it's a little late for all this brown and yellow. The dog has a bloody stump where his tail used to be. No doubt coyotes, like the old man said. The bald man squats down and pets him, examines his wound. Now *isn't* that a nice thing for a big bald man with a broken nose to do!

He sees me, there by the door. He pulls off his hat by one of its earmuffs, letting the sun shine out on his bald head which makes him even more lovable. So not only dark and dangerous, but more polite than need be under the circumstances. He could have just waved.

I don't want him meeting this old man and seeing his odd art, but here he comes, crunch, crunching across the snow. I give another coo. The old man humphs a humph as if: I knew she was us, or, on the other hand: I knew she was crazy.

(Come on in. Rescue me. Take me back with you. I'll keep my voice on an even keel. I'll not singsong. I'll not smile too much. I'll never coo in public. I'll pull my long limp hair back tight and weave it into a bun so it doesn't fly around by itself. I'll not screech when I laugh.)

"Coo. . . . I mean come. Come on in."

"You shouldn't be up here. There's another storm on the way. There isn't much time."

I do love how his voice rattles out from someplace way down deep in his chest.

I lift. I actually lift out of pure joy. I stoop to greet the dog at the same time as I lift in order to hide it. It must have looked kind of funny, down and up at the same time.

That bald man has to lean over to get through the door, and there's hardly room inside for somebody as big as he is. Even so he wanders back and forth, peering at the "art" close up, touching things. The old man stays in a corner and mutters to himself. He had just asked me if I wanted breakfast but now it's clear he's not going serve either of us anything.

After looking around the bald man takes out his first aid kit and treats the dog's wounds.

After that, the man and I start back down, first through trees, but then the mountain opens out to wide views, all sky with nothing in the way of it. We like the "big sky." Hard to explain but I like this man for exactly the same reason.

I want the storm to catch us. I want us holed up behind a rock or under a tree so he'll get to know me. I lag behind and he keeps saying, "For Christ's sake hurry up. Look at the clouds rolling in." To slow us down even more, I turn and look and right behind me there's two perfect stones next to each other, and just room enough for a foot between them. I do it. I step in and twist.

It hurts more than I expected. I did a good job of it, my pants are ripped and my boot is all scratched up, but then I get to have his big warm hands all over my leg and foot. He has everything he needs in his first aid kit. He tapes up my ankle in a sort of figure eight, and as stiff as a cast so it hardly hurts at all. (Luckily we never get the misshapen feet all ballet dancers have.) After that I get to have his big warm arms around me as he carries me to a better place than on this slippery snowy slope.

That's what he *says* he's doing, but he's got ideas, too, just as much as I have. We don't make it off the slope. As he carries me, he slips. On purpose. I *think* on purpose. We slide down a long snowy bank and would have gone over the edge of the cliff if I hadn't stopped us with a hard lift. He's so heavy. I don't know how I had the strength for it, but here we are, stopped right at the edge.

He says, "You're one of those others."

"What others?"

"Don't try to fool me."

So he does know. I say, "I saved you," to distract him.

He twists my arm, but not too hard. Just a little warning. He could have broken it with no trouble at all. For sure he likes me.

We ought to move back. I'm too used up to lift again for a while and we might go all the way over and *then* what? I try to squinch myself back, but he holds me. I love his hug, but I'm scared.

"I'm scared."

"Tell me who you and that old man are and what you're up to way out here in the middle of nowhere? What's he making? What's all that stuff?"

Nobody ever tells me anything. They never did. From an early age . . . as soon as they told me I wasn't them but us, I wanted to understand us and (especially) me. Nobody would answer anything I asked.

Maybe those things all over the place in there aren't art after all.

"I don't know who we are. They told me we were us, but they never said what being us was. They've kept us secret even from ourselves. All I know is there's this one thing—this lift. And besides, I can't do it again until I rest up. We have to move back."

Finally he lets us. It's so steep and slippery I have to crawl. He does too. He pulls me along. At the top we crawl sideways to get over on safer ground, completely away from the slope. I have the thought to push him over the cliff. That's what I should do, knowing that he knows, but I don't do it.

Safe . . . a little bit safer, we catch our breath and I get to have his arms around me again. I'm glad I didn't push him over.

We're both shaky. We hug and tremble. With me the trembling isn't from having just escaped and having just used up all my lift, it's that my face is pushed (I pushed it there on purpose) right into his thick neck. His neck comes straight down from his jaw to beyond his collarbone. He looks like the kind of man who'd say, "Try to choke me," or, "Hit me in the stomach." He'd say, "I'll bet you a hundred dollars you can't hurt me." *I'd* bet him a hundred dollars he's said both those more than once.

There's a sudden darkening as if already dusk. There's wind and snow. Just like that, the storm starts. He carries me yet farther back, and pulls me under a tree whose branches come to the ground on all sides. We sit, hugging. I'm still breathing into his neck. He's as shaky as I am. Now why would a man who loves storms and all sorts of dangerous things be trembling so?

Now his hand is on my breast. He's taken off his gloves and reached inside my parka. His hands are large and shapely. I noticed that before. I've always liked good hands. And now those very hands are all over me.

"Actually you're not so different from everybody else."

I'm worried because our breasts are smaller. I say, "But I am different." I'm thinking mostly of my breasts.

"I don't care."

Maybe breasts don't matter that much. Maybe he really doesn't care.

Green pine boughs surround us and beyond them snow comes down. A real white-out. The whole world has turned my favorite color. We're cozy in here under the branches. His knees are threaded in with mine. Our feet, in our big boots, are clumped up together. I take off my gloves and put my hand on the sweaty back of his neck, under his scarf. He's damp . . . radiating. . . .

We kiss. How warm his lips are even now in this snow storm. How soft . . . soft generous lips. (I noticed them before, too.) You wouldn't think they'd be so soft with such a hard muscled man.

He needs a shave, but I don't mind getting scratched up. And I only have a few twinges from my ankle.

"Coo," I say, a long low, "Coooooooo."

The storm is making a racket, branches scratch against each other, the wind whistles, but I couldn't be warmer. I couldn't be more enfolded, engulfed, enclosed. . . . While I coo and squeak, he grunts and growls and bellows.

Now how did this happen?

We sleep. His fuzzy chest is still bare and my ear is still right on top of his heartbeat. It sounds out louder than the wind whistling around us.

At first he's nicely relaxed, but pretty soon he snores and snorts and jerks. The storm does the opposite, it quiets and soon a full moon shines out. It's even fairly bright in here under our branches. I can even see how long his eyelashes are. I noticed them before. I noticed everything before.

I should be thinking about how to get rid of somebody who knows for sure about us, but how can you do that to a person when you've heard his heart beating under your ear all night long?

We can't marry one of you. That's unthinkable though I've thought of nothing else. There have been times when I pretended I'm one of you—what I've wished for since I met this man. When I thought of being you, I flitted down the sidewalk, skipping myself over chewing gum and spit, in a way that could only be us. But we're a dying breed. If we don't take care we might be gone altogether.

Those who aren't careful (those who risk, loving the wrong person) meet with an accident. I mean from our own kind. There's one of us in charge of that. We don't know who. Maybe it's the old man who rescued me. But out here I suppose I'm the one in charge. I should get rid of this man before that old man comes along and kills us both. Or one of us, depending on whether he's us or you.

We wake at first light. We lie in each other's arms, listening to snow melting sounds. That is, I do, but he's been thinking. "What about. . . ." he says, and grunts. I'm hoping he's going to say, What about the two of us? but he says, "What about all that . . . stuff? I could tell the pieces will fit together into something huge. Could be a weapon or a whole bunch of them."

"It's art."

(Isn't it? Does it really fit together into one big dangerous thing? And even if it does, why isn't that art? Art is more important than some device or other for the end of your kind . . . or my kind.)

"It's *art!*"

But he's not convinced.

"If you care for me at all, you'll take my word for it. It's art."

"It's not even beautiful."

"Nowadays nobody is so. . . ." (I almost say, un-sophisticated, but I stop myself in time. He already feels unartistic compared to me.) "Nowadays nobody thinks art has to be beautiful. It's to make us think. Besides, beauty is learned."

"Maybe."

But I want to make him feel good.

"Rescuing is more important than any art could be, though art takes just as much courage."

"I'd like to see what those things look like put together."

"Even if it all fits together why can't it still be art?"

I *want* it to be art. Your kind or our kind, I don't care which. We need more art and fewer weapons. Though, on the other hand, maybe we have too much art. It's hard to keep track of. Hard to sort through. I'd prefer less. But I would never say that in front of him.

He kisses me. A long wet kiss. For no reason at all.

I say, "Marry me."

He looks at me—those glittery black eyes—just looks. He could at least have said, Maybe.

We come out from under our tree into a world of shine . . . white, with blue sky above. I'm *so* happy. (Except that he didn't say, Maybe.)

The man looks all around and then looks all around again with his field glasses. He drops on one knee, ducks partly behind our tree, hands the field glasses to me and points. There, behind us, is the old man. He's sitting on a boulder, looking all around with *his* field glasses. He has a rifle across his knees. And here comes his dog, right to us. Wagging what's left of his bandaged tail.

If only I had a clue . . . one little real clue as to which this old man is, us or you, and whether all that stuff is art or a weapon. If I should yell to that old man, Don't shoot, I'm on your side—I want to know which side that would be.

My man (I'm thinking, My man, though I'm not sure if he is or isn't) says, "Stay here," but I'm not going to.

He starts up the slope, walking boldly in spite of the

rifle across the old man's knees. My man is fearless. I knew that before.

I scramble along behind him, lifting a little so as to save my sprained ankle.

The old man, looking right at us, yells, "Stop or I'll shoot." I don't know if he means he'll shoot me, clumping along behind, or my man. Neither of us stop.

My man doesn't have any weapons. He just has his first aid kit and ropes and things for rescuing people. He wouldn't care if you were us or you people or a skunk or a mountain lion, he'd rescue you anyway.

"Grab him," the old man yells. "Push him. Let him fall over the cliff before he destroys my work."

Now I know which he is.

No I don't, I just know which of us he wants to get rid of and why.

I yell out, too. "He rescues people! That's all he does. He'll rescue you if you need rescuing."

"Not me. Never one like me."

"He has no weapons."

The cold or snow or something (maybe it's the bowl shape of the mountainside) gives our words an odd hollow sharpness—an extra clarity. Words as if in silhouette. Even my big man's gravely voice sounds out with purity.

I see my man's breath as he shouts up the slope. "Don't shoot. We'll talk."

"Push him. He wants to destroy my work."

He's right to worry. You always . . . *always* do that: throw art off cliffs, roll it into the sea, burn it, knock it to pieces, chop it up, smash it. . . . You people cut off marble penises and grind them up for aphrodisiacs. You people threw the Mayan statues down their long stairways. You scraped off the faces of kings you didn't like. You burned codices. Makes me think it must be art for sure if somebody wants to destroy it.

Though on the other hand you people invented all these arts in the first place. We didn't even invent ballet.

By lifting harder, I'm now up beside my man. He's still

clumping through the snow, but if he could stride, that's what he'd be doing.

The man shoots, but my man doesn't go down. Just keeps slogging along. I'm the one yelling, "Don't shoot," and everything else I can think to yell. "Stop. Please. Don't."

The old man stands up and starts down towards my man. My man walks up to him and then right on past, not paying him any attention. I think to attack the old man myself but I don't want to leave my man. I get between the old man and my man. The old man points the gun at me but doesn't shoot, just follows. So here we go, all of us and the dog, back to the shack. And there, just inside the door, my man squats down and takes off his gloves and takes out . . . is that his little camp stove? And then I see he's set the place on fire. But he's a fireman!

I say, "This is burning books. Isn't this like burning books?"

"It isn't art!"

He steps away and pulls me with him, to a safe distance. We watch. The old man, too. Everything goes up, poof, like an old Christmas tree. There's no way to stop it. My man sure knows how to set a good fire.

But *now* . . . just like that, my man flops down and I see blood. It's dripping . . . more than just dripping, out his sleeves. It's all over his hands. The dog licks at them.

I lean over him. I can't believe it. I lean close. I don't see that mist of breath. I don't feel it on my cheek. My big rescuing man is dead. How can this be? And his very last words were, "It isn't art."

I hear my "Nooooo!" echoing all over this snowy bowl. I turn. I don't know how I find the strength but I grab that that wiry old man, and push and push and drag—him and his rifle—all the way down the slope and over the cliff. He yells the whole way, but I couldn't tell you what or even in what language. I can't hear or understand anything. I don't care which he is, us or them.

After, I sit with my feet hanging over the edge. Sit and sit and sit, not thinking. Pretty soon I go back to sit by my man. I guess I can say he's mine now. He can't say he isn't. By now the fire has burned itself out some and the sun has gone behind the mountain. I guess I sat there, on the edge of everything, longer than I thought. I'll have to spend the night here just sitting, but it's what I want to do.

I push the dog away. I take off my glove and hold my man's cold, bare hand. How could such a warm furnace of a man? How could?

At first I just sit and don't think at all and then I do, and hope. If what I hope is true, it's already too late to keep our purity untainted by you people. But I don't know what to think anymore. I've been *so* careful. I've even danced cautiously, all the time thinking: Stay down. I'm tired of it.

I'll leave the ballet. Take the tailless dog and leave. I'll join the circus. It's good for us to be in the circus, we're so much safer there. If we lift by mistake, everybody thinks it's some trick or other. I'll hang on by my teeth and get raised to the top of the tent. All of us can do that, no trouble at all. Tightrope walker might be nice. I could have a pink parasol.

Except, if I'm pregnant. It'll be hard when I have to lift for two.

I can't be sure for a while yet, but I want a little black haired boy with big feet and hands and long eyelashes. I don't care whether he can lift or not. When he climbs a tree and falls, he'll come straight down like everybody else does.

It never would have worked. I don't think he liked art much, anyway.

Form follows function? Beauty? Truth? Those are old notions. Besides, *we've* never lived with much truth. We can't. We don't even try. But there's all kinds of reasons for art.

His very last words were, "It isn't art." He never said, I love you. He never even said, Maybe. I wonder what he meant by not saying, Maybe.

THE ASSASSIN
～ OR ～
BEING THE LOVED ONE

✑

I HAD BEEN SENT to assassinate the general of the opposition, but I didn't do it. I had him in my sights, but instead I let him shoot me.

I had promised to do it or die trying. I was dying, but I hadn't tried. I had looked into his eyes, then looked into the little black hole of his weapon, knowing he was looking into mine. I had even said, Sorry. Suddenly, I *was* sorry. Then I hadn't done it. I had the thought there might be something lesser I could do, something appropriate like cut off his trigger finger. Or better yet, cut off his thumbs.

He had a big grey moustache and blue eyes. His face was brown and weathered. He looked exactly like my father even to the squinting eyes. In fact for a moment I thought it was my father, grown older and come back from death, and somehow switched over to the enemy's side.

This general was walking in the very mountains where the battles had taken place. I knew these hills as though I'd grown up here, and I'm sure the general did, too.

The war was over—said to be. Treaties had been signed—a whole year ago, but what did that have to do with us? If *we* didn't want it to be over, it wasn't. And we weren't the only ones. There were many pockets of holdouts. The war had gone on for ten years. We couldn't figure out why we should stop now. What had changed? We promised each other we'd keep fighting one way or another until we were all dead. But there are few of us so we have to make our killing count. We didn't want to kill just anybody. We went to the top.

Certainly this general thought it was over or he wouldn't have been on the trail with his three grandsons. Nor would he have been in mufti. I knew who he was from the posters of victory, and I knew which cabin in the foothills was his summer home. I knew he had three grandsons and that his only son had been killed in the war. He looked so much a civilian, I was surprised he carried a pistol.

I had followed them all morning until the children and their terrier fell well behind and the general was already on the switchbacks. He was going fast. He obviously loved working himself hard. He obviously thought there was no danger to the boys.

I hoped not to kill in front of the children—though it might be a good lesson for them. I thought perhaps I could shock them with the shooting and then capture them for our side. There aren't many of us left. They were young enough to be convinced to change sides. We were, after all, the side of the upright. (When had we not been? We'd have changed sides if we thought we were wrong.) But if we couldn't convince them then their thumbs could go, too.

As the general climbed, switching back and forth, I took a shortcut. I ran straight up, turned around at the top and waited for him behind a boulder.

I had not realized he was a small man until he rounded the corner of the trail, came out from behind the cliff, and stood not more than six or eight yards from me. I had not seen his face close up until then.

The force of his bullet spun me to the side. I slid down a long bank of scree. I lay at the bottom knowing nobody would come to help me. I was done-for, way out here in the middle of nowhere.

I felt no pain. I stared up into a gnarled juniper. One doesn't often look straight up, along the trunk of a tree. It's a whole other view. I was charmed. It was a revelation. The branches hardly moved. It was a puzzle I could solve. A magpie sat in the puzzle for a moment. It gave a magpie kind of quack. I thought he was trying to tell me something. Perhaps announce my death to the rest of the forest. I thought how beautiful everything was. There was sun and shade, back and forth over my eyes, so now and then I couldn't see for the brightness shining through.

And all the time I held my hand against my head, hoping to stop the blood, but I gave up. Then I began to die. I could feel my life flowing away. It seemed all right. I didn't have the energy to live, anyway. I was glad I didn't have to get up and do something. I had let my comrades down but I was glad nothing needed to worry me ever anymore. It was over.

But it wasn't.

I wake in a small white room with bars on the window. I'm alone. My head is bandaged. My first thought is of escape. My second that they should have tied me up. Then I think I must hurry to take advantage of the fact that there's no one here. I jump up and fall flat. The floor is cement. I hit my forehead but my bandage helps to shield me. I have to wait a moment to recover and then I crawl to the window, pull myself up by the bars, and hang on to keep myself standing.

What at first seemed like snow is apple blossoms. It's a garden out there, lawns and flowerbeds, pathways. There's a fountain with the statue of a naked girl in the middle of it. To one side, a naked boy looking up at her, makes it look unbalanced. It seems a place especially made to cheer those wounded in mind and body. I'm full of yearning. To be in the sunshine and the blossoms, that they should be blowing down on me—to look at the naked girl.

I shake the bars. Hard. And harder. I hear myself grunt. I sound like a bear. Or, rather, what an imaginary bear sounds like. I've seen them on the mountains but never heard more than a sort of cough of warning.

I turn to the door. There's a little window in it. Perhaps I've been spied upon even as I fell and then went to rattle the bars. It's locked. They locked me in. What is this place? I look out at a hallway. There doesn't seem to be anybody around but I can't see very far. There's a painting on the wall, of wild flowers from the area, paintbrush and lupine, asters.

I sink to my knees with yearning for the garden.

When the door finally opens I'm in the way. She almost trips over me. A nurse. She calls for help, but calmly as though for help getting me back to bed. Even so I panic. I'm by her feet. I grab her ankles. She goes down—as hard as I did when I first got up. But she goes down on her chin and knocks herself out.

I start crawling down the hall. It's lined with nature paintings. They're trying to make everything nice—for prisoners? For crazies? I'm tempted to stop and look at them but I want to get out into the real thing. I get up, wobbling. I manage to walk, supporting myself with my hand on the wall. I'm not thinking escape, I'm thinking: Garden, apple blossoms, a fountain with a naked marble girl. . . .

I'm not in pain. There's only this weakness and shaking, and I'm not thinking properly. I know there are important things I should be doing. There's a lost war I'm supposed to be fighting. I think how I had the chance at their general and didn't kill him. One of my friends may die trying to do what I didn't do.

Then I think: Was there a stream? How nice if a stream. I'll sit on the bank. I'll lie in the grass and look up along the tree trunks again. Birds will come. Perhaps another magpie.

I'm wobbling worse than ever. Everything is wavy, the hall stretches and shrinks. There's a door at the end of it. If I'm going to collapse, and I am, I must do it where I'm hidden and preferably outside.

The door is heavy. I have to use all my weight. Outdoors, I fall down four steps, then crawl, squashing pansies, into the lilacs beside them. I feel again the joy of not having to stay awake—not having to do anything. Back in our caves we were always on guard. I was always too tired.

But then women come and sit on the steps above me. I can't see them, but I can hear them. They sound young.

("They just lost a patient." "Somebody died?" "No, you nut, I said, lost. They say he's crazy. They couldn't keep him covered up and they couldn't keep his bandages on." "Is he crazy-dangerous?" "Yes. They say he wanted to kill the general but the general shot first.")

No, no, that's not how it was. I saved him. If not for me he'd be dead. And I'm not crazy.

It's important that they know I decided not to shoot. But I haven't the energy to say anything.

("They're *all* crazy." "They ought to be locked up." "They shouldn't be here. They ought to be in prison." "If I find him. . . .")

She must have made a gesture.

("You couldn't." "Sure I could. I still can." "Knowing you, you'd fall in love. Look at that crazy baldheaded guy you fell for just because he kept staring at you. He stared like that because he was crazy!" "I've got more sense than that. Besides he was one of *them*. And look at *your* guy." "Oh Beth!")

Beth!

I love their voices and that name. It's been so long since I've been this close to anybody female. I want that laughing and that youth. I'm not so old myself. The one who liked bald heads . . . her voice was low, not like some women. I'm not much to look at, but at least I'm not bald. I need for them to know that, except for me, their general would be dead and those three boys stolen away to our side.

If I had the energy I would get up and tell them I saved him. I'd say, under all these bandages I'm not bald. And that I want to love. And I want to be the loved one.

I drag myself out. They jump when they see me. They're

109

both beautiful. I knew they would be. I could tell by their voices. One is dressed as a nurse. That one has long black hair put up in a bun under her little cap. The other has freckles and curly reddish hair as short as a boy's.

I can't stand up, but I rise to my knees. This isn't the time for a speech but I do it anyway. "We've never been otherwise than kind. I saved the general out of kindness."

The one that's not dressed as a nurse is staring at me in horror. Then I see she has no thumbs.

We always thought that was a good idea—the cutting off of thumbs. We thought it was kind. Other groups have cut off hands and sometimes feet. We don't ever do that. We wouldn't consider those.

She should be glad she only lost her thumbs, but she comes towards me in a fury. As if to choke me. I wonder if she can, with those hands. The other tries to hold her back.

"Stop! Beth! He can hardly stand up, for heaven's sake."

I have more right to be angry than she has. They called our triumphal arch their own and made us march through it as part of *their* victory parade. We were torn and dirty (that's how they wanted us to be) while they were all cleaned up and dressed in their best. We were forced to march over our own banners. Behind us, in our beat-up trucks, were our captured weapons. They sang songs of victory. Their trumpets sounded the charge. Their drums beat death.

They thought it would teach us a lesson. It did. We'll never surrender.

Beth finally gets free of the nurse and attacks me. She's stronger than I ever thought a woman could be. Or perhaps I'm weaker than I usually am. And she knows how to fight. She's been a soldier. She knows all sorts of tricks. She's on top, kneeing me in the wrong place. Her fists still work fine as fists. I curl up.

There's yelling. Orderlies come with needles. Not for

her, the one attacking, the one going absolutely crazy, but for me and I haven't even been fighting back. I'm just all curled up.

Next thing I know someone is saying, "Son, son," and trying to wake me up.

I'm in pain, which I hadn't been when there was just the wound in my head. Now I ache all over.

"Son!"

I open my eyes. It's the general. Leaning over me.

Is he calling me his son or does he call all younger men son? He's holding a straw to my lips. He's right, I'm thirsty. I could love him just for this drink of cool water. I could almost change sides for such pleasure.

He looks like a farmer, weathered, lined face, hands scared and swollen from frostbite. I recognize it all.

I wish he hadn't said Son.

Then he says, "My assassin," but he doesn't say it in a bad way. He puts the glass down and holds my wrist. The skin of his palms feels rough—like a farmer's.

"Son, what's your name?"

"___"

"I need to know what caves you come from."

"___"

"The war is over!"

"___"

He shakes my shoulder. "It's *over!*"

"___"

"Long as you're in those caves, nobody is safe. We'd smoke them out. They won't be hurt."

They call that snuffing. "Go ahead. Cut off my hands."

He snorts and lets go of me. Goes to the window. He's looking out at the garden.

"Smoke! You'd burn them out. And you think they won't come out shooting?"

The dark haired nurse is there. I'd not noticed her before. I need for her to know I saved the general. I raise myself on my elbows. "Tell them I saved you." I yell it. "I didn't shoot. Admit it. I saved you."

He turns back towards me, thinking.

"Remember?"

He's thinking back to when we stared down each other's gun barrels.

"I didn't shoot. That was on purpose."

"May . . . be."

He doesn't know what to believe. He turns to my garden, to my naked girl, and I lie back down.

There's broth. The nurse is about to hold the straw for me, but the general comes and takes it from her. Sits down again to hold it.

"Could be. You waited, I did see that."

To him the war is really over. Easy to think so when you're on the winning side.

"You could come up with me and help us get your comrades out. They'd come out for you."

"But then what?"

"Just the two of us? Just get their weapons."

"That's what you *say*."

The window is open. Even here, from my bed, I can feel the breeze. I can smell the lilacs. "Is somebody out there singing?"

The nurse says, "Oh, that's Beth."

"I want to go into the garden. If only for a moment."

"Take him out as soon I leave."

"Can I take his bandage off? I don't want Beth or the other patients and orderlies to know who he is. I'm afraid they might attack him."

"Do it."

Then he tells her, "Take good care of my assassin." He squeezes my shoulder and winks as if we were in this together.

After he leaves, the nurse takes the bandages off and puts on two smaller ones.

They've shaved my head because of my wound, but also my beard. In our caves it's hard to find ways to shave. We were proud of being hairy. It identified us as wild mountain men who would never surrender. We were even proud of being dirty.

I tell the nurse to bring me a mirror.

I'm shocked. I look so old and worn out and starved and sick. I'm greenish under my tan, and there are circles around my eyes. I have to watch myself touching myself to make sure I'm me. I wonder if my comrades would recognize me. The general and I could go up to the caves to bring them out and they wouldn't know me anyway.

"Can you walk to the wheelchair?"

I'm so shocked by how I look I wonder if I can.

"Don't you want to go?

"Come on, it'll do you good.

"I have other patients. I can't wait all day." She says it, even so, with tolerance. She would wait.

I walk to the chair. I'm much stronger than I was before. I tell her I want to be near the fountain.

It is beautiful. Even better than I expected. Blossoms are still blowing down. They're all over my lap before we even get to the fountain. Birds. There's one little bird with red on his head. Maybe a finch. The birds around our caves in the mountains are different. Juncos and jays. The nurse pushes me right next to the naked marble girl and leaves. Across from me, on the other side of the fountain, is Beth, still singing to herself.

There are only a few people around. Some on benches, some in wheelchairs, wrapped up tight, as I am, but except for Beth, I'm the only one near the fountain. If she looked right at me she'd not recognize me without my turban of bandages.

She doesn't pay any attention to me. She sits on the edge of the pool, leaning, with her mutilated hands in the water. I wonder if they hurt and if the cool soothes them.

I watch her. If she's the one fell in love because of being stared at, maybe she'll fall in love with me. But she pays no attention. I'm just another of the patients. I suppose she is, too, though her hands seem healed. She sounds happy right now, but I know she's not. I saw the rage and horror underneath.

I listen to her and to the splashing of the fountain. The sun glitters on the droplets and the pool is almost too bright to look at. Here with the naked girl beside me and Beth leaning across from me, I should feel happy but my thoughts are on thumbs.

I think how it might be. You can't choke people. Can't peel potatoes. Hard to cut your meat. Hard to raise your glass. Can't screw things in. Can't tie your shoes. Would it be hard to hold a pistol? Some ways, having only one hand might be better than no thumbs.

But we didn't do that to just anybody. She'd have to have been a killer, too.

Maybe we found her assassinating one of ours so we made it hard for her to do it again.

Beth hasn't looked at me once. I want to do something to make her see me.

I throw the blanket aside and get up—too fast again. I almost fall in the fountain, dizzy. But then I jump in. I don't know what I think I'm doing. Making Beth look at me—at least that.

The water is over my knees and icy enough to make me gasp. It must come straight from the mountains. The cold wakes me out of my craziness. Why did I do this? I could have just called to her. They said I was crazy. Maybe I am.

Beth jumps in, too, splashes across to me and pulls at my clothes with her thumbless fists, to get me out of there.

"Are you crazy? What are you trying to do?" But then she gets that look you have for *really* crazy people. Like you have to be careful what you say. She says, "You're fine. You have a headwound. That makes your thinking muddled. You'll be fine."

She helps me into the wheelchair as if I'm a sick old man and starts to wheel me back.

"I *have* to stay in the garden."

"You have to get dried off. I do, too."

"Please wait. It's not cold. I don't know when they'll let me come out again."

"Well. . . ." She sits on the edge of the pool next to me. "Maybe for a minute."

"I haven't talked to anybody since I came here. I mean really talked. Please."

She leans close to me, tucking me in. Obviously she doesn't know I'm the one she attacked. She has apple blossoms in her hair. I'm in love already. Not that I wasn't back when I first saw her—felt her, bony, against me.

"I like your singing."

"I used to sing."

"Did they do this to you because you were singing enemy songs? People have done things as ridiculous as that but I didn't think we ever would."

"I was a bodyguard for the general. He's my uncle."

I ask her what her name is, though I know it already. I say, "I'm Len." I really am. I won't tell the general, but I tell her.

It turns out she's been helping in the hospital ever since she was here for her mutilated hands. "I'm more trouble than I'm worth, but I try. They let me think I'm helping."

She's sitting so close our knees touch now and then.

I never believed in that heaven for old soldiers, though some did. I begin to think it's really true and this is the maiden assigned to me, just the kind I like the best. And it smells so good of damp earth and new-cut grass. Reminds me of haying time. But if a heaven, why, then, is my wound still here, my bruises aching, and her thumbs still gone?

"I could stay out here forever. Maybe this is forever. Maybe this is heaven. I hope it is."

"Don't count on it."

"After all, I did die back under the juniper. I thought I did."

I see her suddenly understanding.

"It's *you!*"

I brace myself to be attacked but she sits quietly.

"It *is* you!"

"What did you do that we did this to you? There has to be a reason."

"You did a lot more than just cut my thumbs."

I know what she means.

"I'm here now partly because of that. What *you* people did. Not so much because of thumbs, though that, too."

She gets up but I grab her wrist. "I would never."

"We were just the enemy. We weren't even human. We were dirt under your boots."

"What do you think we were to you? Even now, you hunt us out and call us rock rats. But I didn't. I wouldn't."

Actually I never had the chance. I might have. We thought of them as hardly human. We said they ate grubs and rats. We said they copulated with animals. But I was never sure if that was true.

She tries to pull away but I'm strong now. I can hold her. "Please. I would never. I wouldn't."

"There's no kinder man than the general and you wanted to kill him."

"But I stopped myself right in the middle. He'll vouch for that. I let him shoot me. Ask him."

She stops struggling. She's so close to me. I'd hug her if I dared, but then she'd think I was one of those others that raped her. She already thinks I'm like them.

I let her go. I think she'll leave but she doesn't. She sits back on the edge of the pool, hunched into herself.

"I've believed in my uncle from the beginning."

She speaks softly and with lots of hesitations.

"I was a private guard for him. Your people captured me. You almost killed him that time, too. You killed two guards but you took me for . . . other things."

I wonder why she's telling me this. You'd think she'd be attacking me again.

"It wasn't me."

I want to comfort her. I reach to touch her arm. She flinches but then she lets me. Just touch. I don't dare do more.

"After I escaped I tried to assassinate your leader. I

didn't kill him, but it wasn't for lack of trying. That's why you cut me. Somebody else killed him later."

That was the beginning of our end—losing our leader. That sent me into the mountains to become a wildman. But at least she didn't do it.

"I was crazy when I came here. I'm not quite so crazy anymore. But I'm still crazy. I can't look at you."

Though she's looking.

"You're cold. Come on, I'll take you back."

She tucks me in tighter. Holding the blanket with her fists. I feel bad that it's so hard for her to do everything, even this pulling on my blanket. Her hands are long and slim and brown. They're strong and beautiful at the same time. She's kind, even to the likes of me.

"Can I have some real clothes?"

"Where would you go?"

"Am I a prisoner? My door was locked."

She hesitates. Too long. Says, "No." Then, "Of course not." She's decided to lie.

Maybe this is an insane asylum. It is! Beth said she was here because she went crazy.

I look around to see if the garden is walled but I can't tell. There's so many trees and hedges. There *is* a stream. I can see it shining in the distance.

"Don't lie. This isn't a hospital, this is an insane asylum."

She doesn't know what to say. "It *is* a hospital, but . . . and. . . ."

Just then the general comes again. You'd never know he was a general. He's wearing a wine-colored shirt, sleeves rolled up and neck open. He's striding along like he did on the trail.

He hugs Beth hard. He's no taller than she is. He looks at me over her shoulder as he does it. I feel he's reading my thoughts. It doesn't matter if he is because I'm glad to see him in spite of myself.

Beth says, "This is Len."

"Ah hah."

He's brought me a present. A basket of fruit. It's a bribe.

This whole place is. All these people being nice, as if trying to change my mind.

He sits on the edge of the pool beside me, gets out his pocket knife and begins to peel an orange.

We never were able to have much fruit up in our mountains. Even the aroma. . . . It's a bribe that's working.

"Son."

Not that again.

"Don't you think it's time for your friends to get out of those caves and start living their lives? Aren't you tired of all this?"

"This is a prison isn't it? A place for all the crazies who won't stop fighting."

He hands me sections of orange.

"There are no more military prisons."

"I'll believe it when you give me clothes and let me out."

"We will."

"Even Beth said she was crazy."

They give each other a look. It makes me feel even crazier.

He goes on handing me fruit, not talking, just thinking hard. I can almost see him wondering how to make me give up my friends.

"We'd go up together, just the two of us. After that you'd be free. I promise."

I'll not fall for that. There could be troops coming up behind us. If there weren't, maybe *we* could capture *him*. But I'm thinking: How about Beth and me going up together? What if I escape and bring her with me? Or, better yet. . . .

"I'll do it if Beth comes with us."

"Done!"

What have I gotten myself into? And my friends? Maybe I can go to empty caves and pretend they've left. Maybe we can overpower the general? Would they rape Beth yet again? They would if they had the chance. Would I?

That cave life was all I knew for so long I forgot what life could be. We promised ourselves we would never stop, but I'm tired of it. I want to love the enemy. Marry the enemy. Forget the war.

"Are you up for tomorrow? You can set the pace."

I feel strong. I have the rest of the day and night to think. Maybe gather up a weapon or make one. Even a fork might do damage if used properly.

The general leaves, hugging Beth again and squeezing my shoulder. Beth takes me back and helps me into bed. She looks like a warrior woman but she's so gentle. The gentler she is the worse I feel about her hands.

I finally get clothes—clothes none of my companions would recognize me in. The shirt is much too bright a red. The hat is yellow. The general will be able to keep track of me. He and Beth, on the other hand, are dressed in earth colors. I wonder how I can make my friends understand it's me.

We're traveling light. If the general has a gun, it's hidden. I have an ordinary knife and fork. I'm sure they know they were missing from my supper tray.

We cross the garden on a red brick path. Cross the stream by way of a Japanese bridge. There is a wall—much overgrown with vines. I could have climbed it.

We spend the night at ten or so thousand feet, a few hundred feet below where our caves are. Our army was in shambles so only one cave was still occupied. I'll go to that one last and only if I have to.

It's cold up there at night no matter how hot it was during the day. We huddle into one small tent. All this still seems like, if not *the* heaven, then *a* heaven, even though the general sleeps between us. What if she'd love me?

I dream Beth's hands are whole and mine are mutilated. Hard to tell if it's a nightmare or a wishful dream to save Beth. Then I'm trying to comb her hair. I can't hold the comb. I wake with the general shaking my shoulder. He's calling, "Son. Len. It's all right. The war is over." He goes back to sleep holding my wrist. I feel anchored and safe but I don't sleep right away. I listen to their breathing, Beth's and the general's. I must do something—for Beth. I don't know what.

I have to lead the way now. The general comes last. I hope for a time when he lags behind, but he sticks close to Beth. I want to tell her I'll do anything for her. I want to tell her I love her, and I won't let her be hurt again, but the general is always in the way.

Twice I take them to empty caves and say, as if surprised, that our men have gone, but they see right away that nobody has used these caves for a long time and insist I go to a real site. But when we get to our occupied cave, there's nobody there either. I whistle the secret whistle but there's no answer. We go in. The fireplace is cold. It looks as if nobody's been there for days.

Beth and the general can see this really was our cave. There's even food left here, half eaten by varmints. Now that I've been out of there a while, I can't stand the smell. I'd not ever want to live there again or any place like it full of unwashed men.

But they're on the cliffs above us, my friends . . . my used to be friends. . . . I realize it the minute I hear the landslide coming down. I know them, they'd kill me without a second thought if they thought they could get the general, too. Besides, I did betray them.

I try to pull Beth to the side, but everything happens too fast and I'm too busy trying to breathe.

When things slow down . . . when the landslide's finally just a trickle, I'm covered with gravel. I push myself out from under. I'm scratched and bruised, my clothes are shredded, and I'm practically back down into the foothills. All that hard climbing to get up and I'm down in a minute. But where are they? I try to climb again, straight up the scree, but that's impossible so I climb beside it. Then I try to cross to its other side and almost slide down it again. I hunt all day. At evening I find the general. I free him enough to see he's dead. I can't find Beth.

I'll go for help. If Beth is alive she'll try to come back to the asylum. Maybe she's back there already.

I arrive at the fountain in the moonlight. It's so beautiful. Everything is silvery: the apple trees, the ground littered with silvery petals. I sit on the edge of the pond next to the statue. It's a cold place to sit. I'm shivering.

I hadn't realized before how much the statue looks like Beth, slim with small breasts, a young body. Beth is not that young, she's more my age, but her body is girlish. My warrior woman.

The one boy is on the right. I take my place on the left where there should be another. I make it symmetrical. It's almost as if this spot was waiting for me. My feet are in the icy pond but I want to be there, anyway.

The girl leans as Beth leaned. One hand towards the water as though to soothe the pain.

My God, someone has broken off the thumb! Who would do such a thing?

Her other hand is curled close to her, as though to hide her breasts. I lean up to check it. Someone has broken off that thumb, too.

She's so silvery and beautiful. So cold. I want to warm her. I put my arms around her knees. I look up into her face as the other boy does. I was cold to start with, now I'm colder but I no longer shiver. I won't let go. I grow stiff. I couldn't move if I wanted to. I'm thinking how I've never been as happy as here in the garden. I hope they let me stay.

SEE NO EVIL, FEEL NO JOY

"Joy shines out only to reveal what the annihilation of joy will be like." —COETZEE

IT'S A BRIGHT, SUNNY evening. The view from our porch has clouds, pink and lavender, puffy, over purple mountains. I don't look. I control myself. I keep my eyes on shelling peas. It's against our vows to appreciate any such thing as views. You'd think we'd not have put our huts here on the side of the hill when enjoyment of a view is forbidden. You'd think we'd not have built porches in the first place. You'd think the windows of our huts would be smaller.

I keep my eyes on my work or on the floor or the ground or my shoes. Proper shoes for our kind. Lumpy. As if I'd stepped in mud and it stuck. They're just as heavy as if I had. That helps to make us strong, and we need to be strong.

See no beauty, see no ugliness, see neither good nor evil. Nor hear. See nothing that will take you from your duty. Your simplicity. Nothing that might take your mind off this valley of tears, off this valley of joys.

Keep away from joy or nothing will ever be enough. In any kind of happiness one wants more. There's never enough of joy and beauty.

Suppose we looked out across the valley, we might wonder: Does this beautiful view of ours suffice? Should we climb yet higher to get a better one? Move our houses up there? And then should we look day after day—every morning, every evening waste several minutes? Should we enjoy even the storm? Even lightning on the mountains across from us? Stand at the window as if something might happen even better than is already happening right here? Never get anything done?

We wear black. Our hair is pulled back tight. Both sexes. Loose pants tied at the ankles. We keep our hats and bonnets on all the time. I suppose we take them off when we're in bed, but I only know what I do.

In the beginning was the word, but before the word there were no words.

We've taken vows of silence. Instead of talking we leave notes on the door of our refectory. It's been a long time since I spoke.

Do not shake hands or pat shoulders. Touch nothing except your work.

Twice I've seen someone panic. Scream and screech. I didn't have to help. That's a man's job unless there's no man around. Men are allowed to touch in emergencies. I don't know what happened to her or who she was. We don't have friends. When you're not allowed to talk, you don't get to know people. We don't even know each other's names or sexes.

If we should fall in love then no end to it for desire breeds nothing but more desire.

It's unlikely that we will love. Our hats are always pulled low. Our bonnets might as well be blinders.

But I looked down at the wrong time. Right into someone's eyes. That's all I saw—eyes, looking back into mine. It was a mistake. We were both innocent. We looked away quickly. Maybe not that quickly. We stared. I don't know how long. He had brought a heavy pail of water in. Then he'd knelt and dipped himself a drink. I looked down and he looked up. It wasn't our fault.

I thought: My God, like a sunrise you're not supposed to admire, like the sound of the stream you shouldn't listen to, like the view across the valley to the other mountains. After, I could think of nothing but eyes—greenish gray ones. I could see my tiny self in his pupils.

I peeked at him as he left. All I saw were the usual baggy clothes. Faded black. Whitish in the worn spots. I wondered all the things we're not supposed to wonder: What is his name? What hut does he live in? Of course there's no way of finding out.

I wonder what *he* thought. Something passed between us. I think. I don't know what.

Live and do and be in the spirit of the land and with the labor of the land. Live and do and be as was done before and as we've done and will do.

Do and be. And be in a place where no prying outsider ever comes.

Disobedience . . . that one forbidden glance . . . has made me hum. Someone taps me on the wrist, hard, with a wooden spoon to remind me not to. I deserve that tap.

Ever since that look I've been disobedient in both thought and deed. I've been looking—out from behind my big black bonnet. Which one is he? And will he be looking for me? Out from behind his wide brimmed hat?

It is well known what happened to other sects with no sex. It has been decided that we have to have sex but best not to know with whom. And to only have it just often enough to make sure we replace ourselves.

We won't take in orphans as some sects did. Those children may have been spoiled for us before we get to them. Also it didn't keep those other sects alive. We'll grow our own.

I'm to be the first. I don't know why. Our leader has decided which of the men will combine with me to make the most eugenically perfect baby. I'm to go to the mating hut tomorrow night. They don't want us to have time to think about it but I need to think. I'm not sure I want this. Especially not *now*.

We live empty of desire. All pleasure is too much. It ties one to this world so that leaving it is a calamity.

I run away. Not down to civilization, where all is evil and dangerous—people shoot each other, people fight, the air is polluted, it's noisy, the streets are full of beggars—but farther up, into the wilds—the safe, soft wilds.

When I get far enough away I hum—as loud as I wish. How good it is not to be working in the kitchen. How good to be able to look out at the view, to listen to the birds. At the banks of a little river I stop and sit and do that, just listen. I sit so still a bird comes right to me. A little gray bird with a black head. Almost as dull as all of us are. Yet he's bright and chipper. One can be chipper even if one is nothing but gray and black.

Eyes and hands. . . . I can bring back the vision of the moments we looked at each other. He was holding the edge of the pail with one hand and the dipper in the other. His hands were scarred and rough, as all ours are. His had little black hairs on the knuckles. He raised the dipper slowly. As if as stunned by the view of me as I was of him. I saw something of his gaunt face, the crow's-feet at the edges of his eyes, his beard, streaked with white.

I spend the night lying against a fallen tree trunk. I didn't bring a blanket or a sweater. I didn't plan. I ran off too fast to think of anything even though I'm not to be mated until tomorrow night.

Then I realize I can sneak back at meal times. Who's to know? The way we live, one more black bundle gone off to sleep in the woods won't be missed. Why didn't I think of this a long time ago? I'm going back to find those eyes. I'll go where the men work.

First thing in the morning, I find a bright blue feather. I think that's a good sign. I pin it on my tunic. I must remember to take it off before I go back, though would anyone notice? And what would happen if they did?

Life without words is peaceful. There are no disagreements. One is not led astray. No one mishears or misinterprets. And words can make one unhappy as well as happy. Also there are many words that should never be said.

I practice talking just to make sure I still can. I don't know why, there may never be anybody to talk to. I must be thinking I'll talk to that man.

I haven't talked in so long I'd hardly know what in the world to talk about. There hasn't been anything to say since . . . I can't remember when.

At first nothing comes out at all. Then it comes out suddenly, as a shout. No and then yes. After that a whisper. Yes, yes, yes. Finally I get it right. I say: Listen, look, see. Then I remember nursery rhymes. Deedle deedle dumpling; Higgledy piggledy; One a penny, two a penny, three a penny, four.

Perhaps I would like a child. Perhaps, instead of staying up here, I will go to the mating hut tomorrow night. The male they chose for me has got to be for the best child possible. Probably better than anyone I'd choose for myself.

Going back, I look down on our whole compound as if at a map. The people look like busy black ants from here. I can see good hiding places.

When I sneak back for supper, I leave the blue feather on my tunic.

Pins instead of buttons. Knives and spoons but no forks. Water but no tea or coffee. Oatmeal, corn . . . bread, but no butter. Butter is too blissful on the tongue.

At supper I think how different the world is when one looks out at it. All these bent heads. I watch hands. A few have black hairs just as his did. I look out the window where the wind is blowing the bushes. Everybody leans over their trenchers. My blue feather is safe.

Which of the men was meant for me tonight? I'm not to see him. We're to be as anonymous to each other as we always are.

What will they do when they find me gone? Come after me or forget about me? Not much to forget—one less silent black bundle, one empty pallet, one less trencher.

After supper I walk towards my hut as I'm supposed to, but I go right past, on up the hill where there's my fallen tree. This time I bring a blanket.

Life has been given to each of us. Life at all is life enough.

Giving life. I think about a baby. There's still time to change my mind. I can go back down, but I fall asleep and don't.

Let us lie at night as empty of desire and hope and terror as in the daylight of our lives. Let our dreams be neither sweet nor fearful. Never the cold sweat of the fear of death, nor, on the other hand, the hot sweat of desire.

As far as I can tell, I have not dreamt such dreams. Not even now.

I wake with the birds. I'm far enough away that I don't hear the rooster down below. The little birds up here don't say: Get up and get to work. They say: Listen. Look.

Either I haven't been looking out beyond my bonnet for so long that I forgot what weather is like, or this morning is unusually beautiful. Fog—below, hiding the village, but not up here. Snowy peaks behind me, pink in the sunrise. It was fitting that it was eyes that set me off on this course.

About me not mating, how will they know? Are there conferences? How long will it take them to find out it didn't happen? I'll sneak back later and see what's happening, but there's plenty of time.

Time is our enemy. It leads to thoughts. Do not think.

I see why. I'm thinking all sorts of things and every single one of them I shouldn't.

But I don't know what I want. I only know what I don't want. All our shoulds. All our promises. Our vows. Swearing to this and swearing to that. They don't add up to any wants.

The city below, while called democratic and while people vote for their leaders, is full of poverty, drugs, murders, muggings, greed, spending . . . and spending to no purpose but to spend. Leave all that behind and come to us. Once and for all climb away from all those others and their self-congratulation—from their boasting of their rights of man.
Live as we do here.

Do I live? *Did* I live? Now, waking to the birds, watching the sunrise with nothing to do but watch. . . . My hand on my stomach feels the worn cloth of my tunic. Such softness—soft tunic on top of soft stomach. How have I not noticed that softness until now? Even with my promise not to? And how have I not noticed the tops of trees? And haven't we had these same little birds down where we live? Don't we have a stream?

Do not raise your right hand. Sit in a neutral position. Neither kneel nor prostrate yourself. Make a simple promise

129

to do your duty. A promise in any position should be a promise as good as any other.

Give thanks that we have but little, and for what little we have. For shoes that hold. For a warm sweater. For a blanket. For firewood. Most of all for having been born at all and for this short time on earth.

Time is exactly what I have the most of. Yesterday I didn't know how to use it. Now I pick berries. Nibble at spearmint. And the smell! I'm mostly used to kitchen smells. Now there's a piney, tree smell.

We always bathe in big pans and in our (black) bathing dresses so as never to be naked. I take my clothes off and bathe in the stream. I look at myself. I wonder about my age. Am I too old? For yearning?

I've renewed my vows every first snow without wondering. I've promised over and over to be one of us, pure as mountain snow, and yet, even so, and though I've kept my eyes on the floorboards, I've noticed things: the knots in the wood, the different sizes of feet. I've thought I could tell male from female by the ankles. All this time I've appreciated life more than I should.

I was so young. Now I'm . . . a woman who doesn't even know her age. Still of childbearing age or I'd not have been chosen. Though you'd think by now we'd all be a little old for childbearing. (Do they somehow keep track of those of us still menstruating? I suppose they do.) Maybe this is a last chance. A sudden decision by our leader. Perhaps some of us have died. How would we know? We're kept from pain as well as joy.

No weeping no love no hate no sorrow. . . . Being here right now in a single moment. What can ever hurt? We have done away with yearning and desire. No one is eager for more of anything or for what they don't have. There's neither anger nor anxiety nor greed nor hope.

I *am* greedy. I want to see those eyes again. I want to see those long fingered battered hands. When I see them I'll want to see them yet again . . . and again. They're right, there's no end to it.

I come back down for lunch and then hide and watch—the black bundles at their busyness. They don't look up. Easy to hide. I can even do a job here and there and nobody knows. I head over to where the men work at men's work. There I have to hide because of my bonnet. I wonder if I can find a hat somewhere. I watch from behind the lilacs.

The men are building a new outhouse. It will have four sections. Two for men and two for women.

A black figure in a black bonnet comes with water. They stop to drink. They take their hats off and put water on their hair. They pour it down the backs of their tunics. I leave my bonnet in my hiding place, sneak out and grab a hat. But one of the men isn't watching his feet as he should. He sees me and grunts. It's a grunt of surprise. They all look up.

Will they find out about all the forbidden things I've done? Will they see in my naked face that I fell in love with eyes? That I spent two days and nights doing nothing but listening and looking? Even that I bathed naked? And here's my blue feather, right in front.

They don't say anything, they just stare. Of course. How can a person talk after so much silence? Even I . . . and even after I practiced on the mountain. . . . Good that I did or I'd be as they are, but I *can* speak though it comes out too loud again. I say, "I speak. I have wished and hoped and felt yearning. I don't deserve to be among you."

I peer into faces. I look for gray-green eyes. For a beard with white streaks. But I embarrass them. They all look down again.

A single moment is calm. All single moments are peaceful. Time will hold still.

I see that this is true. There's time to breathe. Time for the heart to beat. Time for a bird to sing. For a bumblebee to buzz. Leaves catch the breeze.

Here, in this long, long, long moment, I think I can move about as I wish. Run away. Nobody will see. But one man is watching. Is he our leader? Or one of our leaders? I've no idea how many there might be.

He's memorizing me. I think about my face. I seem to remember I used to have a birthmark on my cheek. That'll be easy for him to remember.

His eyes are not green-grey.

He comes towards me. Nobody else moves. They're all still looking down. They don't want to see what might happen. It might lead to pain and thoughts.

I see his clenched teeth. He's reaching as though to grab my throat.

I grab the nearest tool. It's a saw. All I do is hold it out, the rough edge facing him. He runs right into it. His tunic sleeves hook on it. There's blood on his arms. Even so he keeps coming, pushing his arms yet farther into the saw. Blood pours out. That stops him. The others look. They see a hurtful thing. They've tried all this time to avoid just such as this.

Keep each other safe. You are each other's keepers. Do no harm.

I didn't mean to. But he looked so angry.

They all go to help the man. I pick up the hat and put it on. It's too big, but all the better. I run.

Nobody follows. After a minute I walk at the usual pace, as if busy. I'm as good as invisible. I loop back to see what happened to the man. I hope I didn't kill him. All I did was stand there. He did it to himself, coming after me like that.

The other men are binding his cuts. I didn't kill. At least that.

There's a nursing hut for accidents or sick people (though out here in the wilds we have hardly any flu or colds). I stayed there when I broke my ankle. Four men carry him there. Others go back to work on the outhouse. I follow with the men but I stay well back.

The lunch bell clangs.

We all go except the four men at the nursing hut and the hurt man.

Later there's a message on the nursing hut door. It says what has been said before.

Life is dangerous and deadly. Unforeseen things will happen, but know that all is well until a later time when all that is, will end, even in the very next moment.

I go back to work with the men. It's much more interesting than women's work. Perhaps because it's different. And then you get taken care of. People bring water and later in the afternoon, women come with a snack.

There are new things to like. The smell of fresh cut wood.

Once I admit it to myself, I did enjoy things. The floor boards, the earth and its weeds, the gruel, the smell of rain. I didn't mean to. It's as if one has a need to enjoy whatever there is to enjoy.

I don't know if I'll get to see those eyes again or not but I'm watching for them and I'm happy.

Focus. There is no moment but this empty moment right now. This moment is enough. It is all you have.

Such a full moment. Man sweat. We don't smell like that. They could find me out by sweat alone. And I keep looking out at everybody.

In the evening after work, the men go down to the river to bathe. I go back and pick up my bonnet from behind the lilacs and put it in a safer spot. With both a hat and a bonnet I'll have more freedom than ever before.

All are equal here, and all equally neutral. All neither happy nor unhappy. Our minds are on what's in front of us. Purity. Harmony. Utility. The only proper life.

At supper the men are looking. Not out the window but at us. They know one of us did it. I make a small slight man, lost in my too-big man's hat. I should have kept my bonnet. And I never took off my feather. Luminous blue. It must be like a beacon.

But only that angry man really saw my face. The others weren't watching when he came after me. They didn't see that he did it to himself. They only saw the blood afterwards. Maybe they think I lashed out at him on purpose.

Do they discuss things? Or do they just know what to do? As: find the woman in a man's hat.

But I see him. I see the hands first and then I look up into the eyes. He's looking right at me. He knows.

Love will make you want to please the beloved. Love will make you want to know the name of the beloved and where the beloved came from.

Above our village I saw beavers mating. I saw birds, the same. They say we mustn't think the word "love." We are not to think more of one of us than of another, anymore than we should value one thing more than another, as why love one spoon better than another spoon.

But it is known though nothing is ever said about it, that one does fall in love even with spoons and cups. Has one's favorites even from among one's socks.

But now . . . right now, if my eyes could speak out without saying a word. If I could. . . . If my eyes could speak. . . .

(Come with me. Up into the mountains. We'll have our own wild mountain children. We'll have each other. Or come with me, even down into the evil of the town. Surely there's a place for us somewhere.)

He looks. His eyes give messages I can't fathom. I can no more guess what my eyes might be saying to him than I can guess at his to me. Mine must be full of yearning.

He looks down and begins to eat. They all do, as if his eating is a signal. Perhaps the signal that I have been found.

Is he our leader? Did I fall in love with exactly the worst one? Or best?

Is escape possible? I stand up and step off the bench, kicking my neighbors in my haste. All those in men's hats get up, too. All those in bonnets sit but stop eating.

There's no sense in running with all those men ready to chase me. I will speak instead of running. I stand up on the bench. That surprises them.

I don't know how I got the courage . . . except that everything is lost anyway.

What I want to say is, I didn't mean to hurt, but. . . .

Words have never made anyone understand anything. Words obfuscate. Confuse. Conceal. Form alibis that sound reasonable, but are just excuses.

I don't suppose my reasons . . . my alibi will sound plausible . . . that I didn't mean to do it. Everyone would say that. If I'm going to use words they'll have to be something different.

"Because I love," I say.

I'm trembling. My voice is shaky.

"Because I love. Because I look out the window and watch the bushes in the breeze. Because I have a feather. Because I watch the birds. Let me go. I'll do my loving someplace else. I confess I've always loved. Even from the beginning. I loved the small bone spoon. I loved the china cup. The apples. Even the beans. Even so, I obeyed."

Everyone watches. They've never seen anything like it . . . like me. Like doing this. They're too stunned to move. If I had run they'd have known what to do. I feel safe as long as I can keep talking. Though I suppose that's not really true. They'll tire of talk.

Then I find myself making excuses. I say, "He ran towards me with his hands out. I was scared. I held out the first thing I could grab. I would never harm another creature. I never have. He looked as if he was going to choke me."

I say, "But I know there are no excuses. I know I am his keeper."

Where does all this talk come from? As if I'd been waiting all these years for just this chance. My voice is more powerful every minute. I've stopped trembling.

I say. "I see that one must see." I wave my arms. I must look as if I'm trying to fly. I say, "There are important things to see."

All eyes are on me.

"Eyes for instance. Are they not worth seeing? Look at each other. At your eyes."

But they don't. They keep looking at me.

"Am I, then, so worth seeing that you stare. After all these years it's only me you see. Look out the window. Your first view should be of clouds."

And there are clouds. It's as if I've called them forth, but everybody still looks at me.

He also. His hands still hold his tin cup. His have got to be musician's hands though there's never any music here.

"I've had enough of feet and floors. I speak. Why not? I look up. I look out the window. I see the lilacs blowing even now."

We are not put on this earth to enjoy. Neither are we put here to feel pain and loss. We renounce them both so as to live empty of all feelings. We learn to control these impulses so as to see the world calmly.

But why are we here?

I say it, "Why are we here?"

I stop talking and wait. They wait, too. Nobody knows what to do.

Before, when someone broke, it was with screaming and crying. That person would be carried off. Nobody knows what happens afterwards. I didn't anyway, though somebody must. But my case is different. I didn't break, I just fell in love. I just began to pay attention.

Then that man . . . the very one . . . comes to me. Holds out his hand to help me from the bench. I take it. It's rough from hard work but warm. I'm holding the long fingers. I can feel his strength.

I step down. I'll do whatever he thinks best.

He leads me away. Perhaps to where they put the people who go crazy. Now I'll find out.

It's just the two of us.

"You looked at me. Remember? After that I began to see."

He says, "We are not put on this earth to enjoy. Nor are we put here to feel pain and loss."

"I want a moment of pleasure. Just a moment of it."

"And after that there's nothing but pain and loss."

"I don't mean a great joy. I mean a moment with both of us, you and I, up the hill, both of us looking out over the valley. Is that too much to ask?"

"All pleasure ties one to this world so that leaving it is a calamity. We live here empty of desire."

"I thought, from your eyes, that you'd be different."

"Do not think."

"But your face. . . . It's kind."

"Give thanks that we have but little."

He takes me to the man I hurt. His hands and arms are bandaged. He's resting quietly until he sees me. Then he looks as if he'd like to try and grab me by the neck again.

My man says, "Life at all is life enough."

I'm wondering which of us he's thinking of. Clearly this man will not die.

"What will happen? To me? Does one have one last wish?"

He begins to lead me up beyond the paths. Where in the world are we going? But I'm happy. How could I not be, I'm beside him, and I'm walking away from the village.

He can see how I feel. He says, "Avoid joy or nothing will ever be enough."

The spot where he takes me is hard to get to. Part of the way it's a scary path on the side of a cliff. He has me go first while he holds the back of my pants to keep me safe.

Beyond the cliff there's a good view. We sit under a tree.

His tree. He headed right for it.

We look out. The view is better than the one from my tree. You can see our whole village.

"You also. You haven't kept your vows. You shouldn't bring me here."

I unpin my feather. I want to give it to him but I see a warning in his eyes. He won't take it. I put it on the ground. I say, "There's plenty more if one is willing to look."

We sit.

"How good it is to look," I say.

We sit.

I ask again. "What will happen? To me?"

We sit.

"I know we can't have those like me in the village. I will remind people of exactly what they don't want to be reminded of. And I hurt one of us. What will the punishment be?"

"We all die."

Is that a clue to what will happen?

"You could leave me here in the mountains."

He turns and looks at me, eye to eye just like that first time. We stare as we did. Again I wonder, how does one read someone else's stare?

"Was the mating I was scheduled for to be with you?"

He stares.

"If with you I'd not have minded."

But I've said too much.

He squints. He frowns. Then suddenly he grabs. Kisses. Hard. Holds me too tight. It's scary. I've never. . . . I don't know what to do. What if that, "We all die," was about what will happen to me in the next few minutes? What if they told him to take me up and get rid of me? What if he thinks to give me one last pleasure?

If that is what this is. It seems done more for himself than for me. He's rough and hasty. Our clothes are bulky, old, and weak. They tear. What then when we go back? If? Will there be enough untorn to outfit one person?

I see him without his hat. Black hair streaked with gray, though not as gray as his beard. I see his hairy body. Sweaty. Strong. Most of his chest hair is gray.

I'm naked and àshamed. I don't know what I look like, to him or even to myself.

"Isn't this against our rules?"

I hope I look all right. I hope I can give pleasure. But he's in a hurry.

And after a moment's rest he does it again.

Am I the dead one so it doesn't matter about me? Except this second time it seems with a little more feeling.

After, do I see something new in his eyes? I'm not sure.

He gets up and tries to piece our clothes into one decent outfit. He leaves me the rags. Says, "Stay here."

Then, just as he goes, he turns and says, "I lost my child. I lost my wife."

I call after him what he said to me, "We all die."

Is this the first time he's said anything that's not part of our doctrine? I didn't know he could.

Have I had my moment? My last request? Was that it?

I put on the rags. Tying and pinning until I'm more or less decent. I won't stay here. I'll go up higher. Except I'm so hungry. First I'll go on down to eat. I could get my bonnet from its hiding place. They're looking for a small women in a much too large man's hat. They'd not notice me in my bonnet, and he won't expect me to have crossed the scary cliff by myself.

But perhaps he was going to bring me clothes. Perhaps even food. He should have said so. Though I suppose one can't expect talk. We're not used to that.

I cross the scary part. Creep into the village to where the men were working. It's late. There's no one there. I find my bonnet and go in to eat. Ragged as I am, nobody notices.

I will not sleep down in the village. I head back to his tree. It's getting dark. I don't dare cross the cliff section of the path. But then I do it anyway . . . start to . . . and I stop right in the middle of the scariest part. I don't deserve to be comfortable. I want to punish myself. I'll sleep here on the edge, a stone for a pillow. It makes me think this is why we shouldn't feel too much. We're all on the edge of a cliff. I'll sleep here as a lesson to myself.

Life is brutal. Life is pain. Life is full cruelty.

Didn't we always say that? And if one loses a child and a wife. . . .

I dream I slash out at everybody with a saw. I dream I killed the man I didn't kill.

I wake up before dawn. I'm yelling. I turn into one of those women who screamed and screamed and had to be led away. But nobody hears me from here. I go on and on until I'm all screamed out. Then I sit on the scary edge, my feet hanging over. I don't feel fear. I don't care if I fall off the cliff or not. I understand, for the first time, what our creed really means . . . has meant all this time. As good as dead. All of us. There's nothing to fear. What could there possibly be to fear?

There are no happy endings. All life ends the same way. Better to live with the knowledge of the end. Every day a preparation for what will, inevitably, be.

Except. . . . Except. . . .

The sun is rising. There's all different reds on the hills beyond. Below, the village is still in shadow. I watch the brightness come, little by little, across the valley floor.

Soon after, I see a black figure, like an ant creeping up the path toward me. It'll take him an hour to get up here.

He looks surprised to find me on the ledge with my feet hanging over. Or maybe surprised to see me in my bonnet. To see my clothes all pinned up. He sits beside me. We don't speak. Of course we don't speak.

He has a bundle with him. Black. After all this sunrise, I'm tired of black. Anything, anything, not to see black and not to be all in black.

He takes out a small package and then puts the bundle beside us. He opens out a little packet and there's bread and lemonade.

I say, "Thank you."

He flinches as if my Thank you surprises him, but keeps silent.

I say, "I've been down home." Though I know he knows that from my bonnet. I say, "I had supper."

No answer.

I say, "But I spent the night right here. There's my stone pillow."

He ought at least to say some of our creed words.

I want to shake him up. To get him to talk I say, "What happened to your wife and child?"

He frowns.

"Tell me."

"Life without words is peaceful. There are no disagreements." And then, "Some words should never be said."

Of course he's right, but I want words.

"What's going to happen now? I suppose you'll take me back."

No answer.

"If we should fall in love, then no end to it."

"There are no happy endings."

"I suppose you want to end it before the end comes."

Nothing.

"So as to know the end."

Not even a nod.

"*Speak!*"

He's squinting out at our valley. I can't stand the thought of going back.

How easy it would be . . . him squatting there, reaching to get more lemonade for me.

"I won't go back."

Of course no answer.

I push him. Off he tumbles, down the cliff. He doesn't make a sound. Of course he doesn't. I look over. I see the black shape below. There's no way he can still be alive. Besides, what would he do with me? Just take me back.

I wait. I watch a long time for movement, but there's none. Though what could I do if there was some? I don't know how I'd get myself down there.

I wait so long I'm hungry again. I open the bundle he brought. There's a man's red shirt. Man's blue pants. A dress . . . a real dress, also blue. A white bonnet with little flowers on it. Where in the world did he get these things? Has he been saving them for an escape? Was he already preparing to leave but didn't know how or what to say?

Desire breeds nothing but more desire.

Was he full of desire?

I sit. I wait. Numb. I don't know how long but I see the sun is low. If I'm to cross the ledge I have to do it now.

I put on the dress and bonnet. I cross and head up, higher yet, into the snow. There's no path. The sunset has spread all across the sky. Everything looks pink. Everything glows. Even me.

GLIDERS THOUGH THEY BE

THEY LIVE, AS WE DO, by the shadows, by the warmth of stones on sunny days, by fissures in rocks. They scramble, skulk, and skitter—as we do. They die, as we do, by the sky, by the trees. Live by black brush, prickly poppies. Die by the drop and dive and skim of the masters from the air.

You'll be right in among them, doing everything their way. You'll be trying to like their kinds of food. You'll be spitting out pinfeathers. In spite of yourself you'll say, Oh, oh, oh. And you'll have to sing their songs of self satisfaction, but don't forget you're one of Us.

Find the ins and outs of their warrens. The windings and dead ends, the escape hatches. Know their ditches, the views from their hills. . . .

They call themselves *The* Creatures, as if we weren't. They call their section of the land, *The* Place as if our place wasn't as much a place as theirs. They say they live at the center of the world as though we don't.

That's all right, let them think what they have to think.

Love your enemies. You'll *have* to. Hide your distaste. But you won't have to kiss them unless you want to. Though sometimes our kind does fall in love with their kind, so soft and pink, so thin, so close at hand, as they will be to you. Our kind always thinks such love is a mistake, but I say, all the better. (You'll be thinking your new babies will take to the air along with theirs. Don't count on it.)

Though they keep calling it that, remember they can't fly. It's only gliding. And their wings ... They aren't really wings, just a few feathers, in with their fur. But they're the big problem. Or, rather, the problem is us ... that we have none. In all other ways we're exactly like them. They crawl around just like we do. Rush from hideout to hideout, all the time looking up to investigate the sky. They squeak out warnings just like we do. We might as well be them though they wouldn't have us.

Bring a sharp knife. Not to kill—of course not—but to ... *you* know. Be sure to get them just before they're fledged. After that, success will be unlikely. Every single one you cut will be a blow in our favor.

It all depends on them, everything depends on them, it always has. Though now everything depends on you.

We can't imagine what our nubs are for except to show we're kin with them. We never fledge. Maybe we haven't tried hard enough—haven't spent enough time dropping out of trees or leaping after grasshoppers. But who, among our young ones, hasn't broken a leg from trying something foolish that those others can do without even thinking.

Perhaps it's all in the mind and we're not thinking the right thoughts. Or perhaps it's fear of falling that forces them to fledge. Maybe they push their little ones off lower branches—pry their toes up one by one and then push. Or break the branch out from under them. If they fall and keep on falling, they'll fledge soon enough. They'll have to. Being harsher on our own young might be the only way.

Nubs are ugly. Wings ... so delicate, so optimistic ... are lovely. Even so it'll be easy for one of us to hide among them. Wear a vest or hang a scarf over where your wings ought to be and you can pass for them. Go!

They have no trees! That's my first shock. Hills and valleys . . . mounds of loose dirt next to entrances, yes, piles of rocks just like home, and bushes. . . . You'd think they'd have trees. I wasn't told the most important thing. Perhaps they have gnawed them all down as a safety measure—which it surely is. Perhaps they don't ever say, Die by the trees, as we say.

But then I see they do have . . . *one* . . . just one huge tree off in the middle of their compound. It's the largest I've ever seen. They must take great care of it. Keep it watered. We had no idea they lived like this.

I wear a vest that hides my nubs. Thank goodness there are some of them that are of our bluish color. We're larger than they are, but not by much. Perhaps that's why we can't glide. Though why don't we fledge? And why have these ugly nubs in the first place?

I had skittered along with others of their kind. I joined a hunting group, bringing back voles, locusts, beetles. . . . I had nothing hanging from my belt, but many others didn't either. Since I'm bigger than most of them, I thought to wrestle something from one of the smaller ones, but then I thought better of it.

Now, through the gates and into their treeless . . . almost treeless compound. I hope I don't look too surprised as I enter.

It's neater than ours. And in spite of having no trees (except that one) they've made plenty of places for shade and to hide under. Little lean-tos and platforms, prickly poppies are growing right on top of some of them.

Handsome though I am (and especially so in my red vest—or so my own kind tells me) right away they squint at me. Some clack their teeth. Perhaps I remind them of Us. I puff up so as to look even larger though I lose some of my shine that way. I know that's not a good idea, considering I'll look even more like one of Us, but I want to scare them as much as they're scaring me. I become myself. Or, rather, I become Us.

I hum a tune I know is theirs—I *think* is theirs—we always said it was theirs, but what do we really know of them? By the looks of their one-tree land, even less than we thought.

It must have been the right thing to do because a large female evaluates me carefully. She has a reddish cast, pink eyes, lashes as long as her whiskers. Each eyelash and each whisker has three colors, brown, white, and pink. Even though she's one of theirs, she's superb.

With my own, I'd chitter or some such but I don't know what works with them. And I don't want to spark any jealousy among their males or attract attention to myself. But I do clack my teeth a few times.

Females are larger than males, and she is one of their largest. But they're not fighters. They're no good for anything but having children. If cornered or if any little ones are in danger, even if not their own, they become much worse than any male could ever be, but I doubt that fighting will be called for if, when I cut, I do it out of sight.

We, I and the hunting group, advance towards the center of the compound. When we're not far from their tree, I leave the group and enter a burrow—up the lookout mound of loose dirt at the doorway and then down, down, down. Just like home.

Soon I hear singing coming from below. Female singing. When I get deeper and closer I stop and listen. You have to be born to their kind of music to understand it. Same with their kind of dancing, (head bobbing up and down—exactly like a lizard trying to attract a female). Bla, bla, bla goes their poetry. But as I listen to the song I can tell there's a pattern to it, and the voice is delightful: squeaky, and shrill. Were it used as a warning signal, there's none who'd not hear and obey. I feel shivers up and down my spine.

They told me, go ahead, love. Might be the best way to hide. And the best way to find out whether it's our only way to survive. They said, "Some of us, as you are, are handsome and bold. Do whatever it takes. Become them as best you can."

Almost all our compounds have gone over to their side. It may be that we have nothing else to do but pretend we're them, except we don't know how. The how, is my job. (Along with the cutting, which will make them more like Us.)

I step closer and around the corner so I can see. There's a large room hollowed out and the floor covered with glittery jay feathers. What a singer she is! I can hardly believe her high notes. Higher than I've ever heard. Out in the open air her song would carry for miles. I don't doubt but that I may have heard her screeches as far away as from our own land. And what a remarkable size to her! Except for her pink, you'd think she was one of ours. Her wings lie, folded under her arms. They glisten in the glow of the burrow. I wonder, at her size, can she really glide? We've heard that sometimes their females get so big they can no more glide than we can.

I flatten my fur to give it more glow. I enter boldly. Everyone has squatted down but I stand in the back—and stare. I can't help it. Even if I didn't want to, I couldn't not stare—her legs so delicate, her feet so small, the bulk of her, her front teeth that peep out as she sings. I wonder if how I feel shines out from my eyes. But then it's in the eyes of all of them, males and females alike.

I try to approach her after the performance but of course everybody else wants to, too. We do look at each other, both of us half a head above the others.

I think how good we'd look, her pink next to my blue. She must know that, too.

After a bit I see I'm not going to get near her with all those admirers crowding around. I leave. I explore the burrow. There isn't much more to it but the escape hatches. And I feel the need for air after all that emotion.

But just as I come out, the call comes. Almost as beautiful as their singer's high notes. Some other singer on guard duty. Sky alert. We all rush back in. After a moment we peek out to see what's going on. Striped neck, striped tail, speckled underbelly. . . . Quite beautiful actually. Sky folk always are. Already high, the flap, flap, flap. A baby shrieks—and shrieks and shrieks. Somewhere a mother calls out her goodbye—calls out her love. The shrieks get farther and farther away though the mother keeps calling out long after it's useless. But it isn't as if we don't all expect this.

It's over. Everybody comes out. Not a one stays inside. Back with my own we do the same. I mill around with the others. We squeak and pat each other. We clack our teeth. It would be a perfect time for another of the sky folk to get us. They would have to take a big one now that the little ones have all been pushed back inside. Though if they're like our own, there's always one or two who find a way to sneak out some back door.

She's there of course. They're still crowding around her. I wonder if I'll ever be able to get close. I ask her name. "Lee-ah of the far North holes." "Ah, the far North hole's Lee-ah." A name equal to her bulk, her poise, her tiny feet.

Everyone is still looking up. I step around them, working my way closer, patting shoulders as I pass the others. I make sure my vest hides where my wings should be. Closer. Then close at last. I whisper. "Lee-ah of the far North." She smiles—her beautiful smile, gnawing teeth showing in the front. I can see she's glad to see me.

I say, "Except that I've met you and heard and seen your brilliance, a sad time."

"A sorrow." She raises her head as though to bare her throat to me. A good sign. Then says, "And you, from where?"

I bare my throat, too, but I had hoped she wouldn't ask the important question so soon. If they're like us, I have to come from far enough away from her north and yet not be from my own North. I say, "Also the North, but the east of the North."

That's the truth. One step farther up from their North and I'd be at home with my own.

It must be all right because she says, "I do love those from the East North." I know what she means by that.

She shakes her shoulders and spreads her wings a little bit as though to show them off.

I shake, too, and hope my vest still hides my nubs. "I say, "Glorious." I show my front teeth.

She asks if I sing. I say, "No," She says, "It doesn't matter. Not at all." Then, "Will you join the contest? Please."

I don't know what she means and it must show on my face.

"The contest!"

I squint and clack my teeth, not from choice but from nervousness.

"The mating. For all of us. And for me! For me!"

"Of course I will."

"Until then," she says and moves away, magnificently— swaying side-to-side on purpose to lure me.

But I'm too anxious to be tempted to the extent she wants me to be right now. I have to find out what she's talking about without seeming to ask. I worry. We have contests, too, but I already suspect what theirs might be. *Of course* would be. Gliding! Probably from higher and higher branches. That's what that tree is for. Once you really look at it you can see worn spots and claw marks, branches flattened out into platforms. I can't be seen doing that. Or even trying to do that. Besides, I'd break every leg—at the least. I don't have to join the mating contest but I want to.

If I don't do it, I can just hear it. "Lost your wings? An accident? The punishment for some crime? What crime is that, to make you one of the Lesser? Go up north where you belong."

Until I came here, I had no idea they call us the Lesser. Though that makes sense. Except we're so large and strong, and we have such a beautiful iridescent blueness.

For the next few days, as I wait for the contest, I show off by lifting things none of them can. I carry heavy loads for long distances. I feel superior to all of them. And I have managed to get three young ones who can't yet squeak out to their mothers what I've done, and removed their first hints of feathers. That leaves no scar, and leaves them fledglings who will never fledge.

I have an entourage of admirers. Young ones who want to be just like me. Several females want me to glide for them when the time of the contest comes, but I'll stay true to my exquisite pink singer.

I remember when I was small and had heard about these others. I couldn't believe that I was Us and not them . . . I was sure I could glide. A group of us climbed a tree and jumped, squeaking out our triumph. One died, two broke legs as did I. All of us bruised and chastened. Almost all our young males try it. After that we stick to our own contests, broad jump, high jump, skittering. . . .

We try not to let our little ones hear about those others, so like us, until they're old enough to understand we're Us, and that we can't glide no matter how hard we try.

Here, they've been practicing their glides. The handsomest, the youngest, the most fit. I'm all of those, but of course I don't practice. At least not that way. I'm awed by the heights they leap from. I'd be frightened just climbing up that high and looking down. So that's what I practice— just climbing up a bit higher than I'm comfortable. I sit on a branch. I make myself stay there until I've stopped hanging on so tight my limbs hurt—until I've stopped sweating . . . stopped breathing hard. Then I go up a little higher and do it all over again.

I miss the afternoons of Lee-ah's singing. I have to do it then because there's nobody around except a few sentinels. Thank goodness none posted near their tree.

There are two times a day I dare practice, when she sings and in the moonlight. (Though the ground is all in shadows, it's even scarier then.) I get to know the tree so well that I know every branch.

She sings for them everyday at midday. It's the time for a

rest. It's hot and the burrows are cool. Everyone hunkers down in that vaulted cavern to listen. They just leave a few guards outside. That would be a perfect time for Us to get almost all of them in one operation. All we'd have to do is close off the entrance and station warriors at the escape hatches.

When I'm up on the branches, I imagine launching myself into the air, leaping away, as far out as I can to avoid the lower branches, my limbs spread. (I've watched how they do it.) I imagine the glide. It doesn't help to think about it. I feel sicker. I cling all the harder. Besides, I know it's hopeless. And when I practice by moonlight I worry about owls. Almost more than the height. They're so silent. I'd be prey and never know it until I was in the sky.

I'm so busy and exhausted with my practicing . . . my useless practicing. . . . (How can it do any good, I'll never glide.) I'm so busy with myself I've only cut the beginning wings of those three fledglings. I did, though, get better at looking down without trembling and sweating. I can walk across the highest branches with assurance.

Someone must have seen me climbing up and then down again without gliding. As I sit, half-asleep. . . . (I was up much of the night practicing. I was feeling good about myself. In just a few days I had mastered my fear of heights.) . . . I hear someone whisper, hot breath right into my ear, the clack of teeth, whiskers pricking me. . . . He says, "You're not what you pretend." It's one of the guards. I know him, he's usually stationed at the escape hatch of the main burrow. He has a piercing whistle. I've told him how much I admire it. I also said I knew what a hard job he has, standing up straight to watch for so long. But he's no friend. "I know your kind. Always trying to be us. Second best if best at all. Third best. Fourth best. There is no second best to us. Who are you?"

"One of your own."

"A half-breed."

"Of course not."

"Live by the leap. Live by the song. Die by the red tail, or by the great white head. Live by the granary." His red eyes glint in a nasty way. "Or live by someone else's granary."

"Our granary, I suppose."

"Why not?"

"Well, you've got them all now." I've revealed myself. "Are you telling?"

He wiggles his nose as though I'd told a joke. Perhaps I have, says, "I'd rather wait and see what happens at the leaping."

The day of the great flights (they keep calling it flying) dozens of sky folk whirl on thermals so high we can just barely see them. Guards with rock launchers stand by. First aid stands by. Runners with stretchers stand by to rush the wounded to burrows.

The leapers climb, first to the height they've decided is the highest they can safely glide, and then they climb higher.

The leap, the dive . . . the lovely glide, arms out as though sky folk . . . those little shiny wings spread. . . . And if they survive, it's a leap into the breeding pool. Perhaps this glide contest is exactly for creatures like me. To winnow out us lesser ones. Make sure the offspring will all at least glide. At least that. Will all be them and not Us.

All goes well for the first few leaps, but then someone lies crumpled. An eagle drops . . . falls . . . straight down, as they always do, wings tight to his sides, and before the stone throwers can even begin to think to do anything, the young one is scooped up. Again they, and I also, call out, Goodbye and love. Then there's silence. Not just us, but all birds, the jays, the quail, and even the crickets, even the cicadas, even they, feel the danger. And there's still plenty of sky folk circling up there, so high they're mere specks.

Even so, they start the glides again. I thought they'd stop and I was free until the next time. But they cheer each other more vigorously than before. Call out, "Fly, fly, fly," (as if they really could), and with more bravado.

Shortly before my turn, Lee-ah tells me I don't need to go too high. She says she doesn't love me for my glide and she doesn't want me to suffer even one broken leg. She'll love me no matter that they'll ridicule me if I'm the lowest jumper. She says she's not afraid of ridicule. She says she had plenty herself before she learned to sing. Maybe she suspects. Maybe she already knows all our offspring will be lesser ones. She doesn't need to see me leap . . . or rather not leap . . . to prove it.

I wish she'd told me this before. It might have made a difference.

I'm fearless. Even more so, here in front of them all. I climb higher than any of them have dared. I might as well. To one like me there's no difference, high or even higher. I look down on them . . . at all those who call us the Lesser ones.

If I'm quick. . . . If I'm clever. . . .

Many shake their heads as though to warn me. I wonder how many know.

Lee-ah stands below, her arms raised as though to catch me. I hope she doesn't. I'd kill her if I fell on her. But then she starts to sing and everybody turns to look at her. They're instantly enthralled. They squat down to listen as they always do. She must know what I am. She's giving me a chance. Perhaps I can climb down the back of the tree, come out at the bottom from around the trunk. It's thick as ten of us. Enough to hide me all the way down. But I choose the doom I've already picked out for myself.

My branch is higher, therefore thinner. I've already gnawed it half way though. I won't launch myself out beyond all the other, lower branches, limbs spread, nubs in full view. I want to come down right *on* the lower branches. I bounce on my branch as though getting ready to leap.

I come crashing down, hitting one branch after the other, reaching out to each as I fall. A feat of skill and strength for one of my kind. And I wish my kind could see me. If I ever have the chance to tell them, they'll not believe.

Even as I fall I'm thinking I hope nobody examines the branch. I gnawed it as best I could to make it look as if it broke on its own, but I'm sure it still has my teeth marks.

Actually nobody sees me. Lee-ah is still singing.

The last part of the fall is the most dangerous. Nearer the ground, there are no branches to grab. I'll have to trust my legs. I wrapped them to strengthen them, but it won't help much.

As I fall and grab branches, I break some of their best leaping platforms.

The last drop. The worst. I plummet down. Crash. I'm so shocked, I hardly know what happened. I'm on the ground . . . broken legs for sure, maybe all of them. And Lee-ah, on her knees beside me. Looking up, teeth clacking. From fear or a warning to the. . . .

The hawk drops. Almost into Lee-ah's arms. They rush to save her. They mustn't lose their singer.

But I'm grabbed. I'm whooshed away so fast. So high. The hawk's squawk and the sound of wings drowning out Lee-ah's calling, "Oh love. Oh love."

Higher yet. . . . I see the whole world. I even see my own land. Little dots that are my own kind. Unaware of me. Crawling from hillock to hillock. We all do. Even these others, gliders though they be, do little more than that. Whatever they call it, it isn't flying. The only way any of us, we or they, ever really fly, is like *this*.

I had not thought there'd be so much wind. So much flap, flapping, and shaking, and that it would be so dazzling. So spectacular. I had not thought . . . the world so all embracing. Astonishing. If only I could tell them.

MY GENERAL

I WAS IMMEDIATELY TAKEN with the general though he was an awful mess and had obviously been tortured. I could hardly see what he really looked like. He was lying on the rubble of a ruined basement. The house above had been bombed out so the basement had no roof. They'd thrown a dirty tarp over him. It had been a cold night but at least it hadn't rained.

He smelled as bad as the place they'd thrown him—of urine and vomit and feces. I cleaned him off before I had them load him in my cart. That whole headquarters area is getting to be a garbage dump: rusty cans, oil drums, the remains of fires where soldiers have cooked and tried to keep warm. . . . Of course where they throw the prisoners is the worst.

They'd given up on getting any information out of him. They said he was mine to do with as I wished. We always take them along with us and get them back in shape for our farms. "Don't be treating him too nice," they said. "He's dangerous." They say that every time. Nothing has happened so far and it's unlikely considering the shape they're always in. Besides, most of them are happy to be with us instead of with our men. Of course we're not supposed to take a general. I'm not going to tell anybody back home.

There's something about this one. I don't even know what. Perhaps because he's a general, but I don't think that's it. My husband is a wide man—wide face, wide body. This man is gaunt, and elegant, and has black hair. Even lying there unconscious, he looks sad. You'd think it would take eyes, open, to look so sad.

All our men are off fighting, or, if they're away from the front, they're torturing prisoners or planning new battles. Nobody's helping us on the farms. They haven't for years. The ground on our terraces is rocky. I and my donkey can hardly plow through it. Some things are a lot easier with a man around.

The men flop the general onto my donkey cart and we start back. Nobody has fixed our road since the war began. They fix the roads that go to the front but not the roads to the villages. I was afraid he'd wake up, what with all the bouncing over rocks and potholes. Or die. I checked on him every now and then. Sometimes I go to all the trouble of getting one home and he's dead by the time I drag him off the cart. I wanted to know it before that happened. If it did, I would dump this one off along the way and come back for another. (My old one had died a month ago. Since spring, I've done all the work myself.)

It's late when I get home. Nobody's about. I tip the general out and drag him into my hut. We're allowed to bring them in when they're sick or unconscious. Otherwise they have to stay outside. I take off his general's uniform and put some of my husband's old clothes on him. I cover him with a quilt and put wrapped-up hot stones by his feet. I let him have the place closest to the fireplace. I got him this far alive, I don't want to wake up to a dead man. Before I bank the fire for the night, I burn the uniform, medals and all.

With all those bruises, it's hard to tell if handsome or ugly. Ugly now, that's for sure, what with swollen jaw and lips, and the lumps on his head, but I don't think he was very good looking to start with.

I don't ever let my little girl see the men when they're first brought in all bruised and battered. We always keep the children away until the men are well enough to work. She talks to them. She doesn't know any better. There's no point in telling her not to. Back in my day I was curious, too. Besides, those were the only men I knew. My father was always gone. It's the same old war.

My daughter comes by first thing next morning to say hello. I suppose she really wants to get a peek at the new man. I kiss her and send her away. She has the goats to look after. I haven't seen her father but five or six times since the night she was conceived nine years ago. When he's at headquarters, he picks out a prisoner for me, checks their condition and their muscles, and helps me load them. This time he was at the front. I picked this one out by myself. I don't know why I wanted a general. They're liable to escape or start a revolt among our other prisoners. But nobody stopped me.

My husband said never to take anybody higher than a sergeant. I wonder how good a general will be at taking orders. I chose him on purpose. I wanted to make something happen. I'm sick and tired of the way things are. I hardly know what men are like except for these prisoners.

The men are supposed to sleep out on our doorsteps—after they're well, that is. I always give mine a pad and a blanket. They last longer that way. We usually work well together. Sometimes I wonder if I was born on the wrong side.

I feed the birds. I net a few finches to fry-up whole. I pluck them and singe them. When I sit down to my midday tea, he begins to stir. I watch him wake.

It's the birds at the feeder bring him round. He looks up, suddenly, as though to find finches on the underside of the thatch. He listens to their warbling as carefully as though they were song birds. Then, even with his bruised lips, he tries to imitate the sound. I do it for him. He turns and stares. My husband's eyes are blue. His are black. He seems to look right through me. His eyes are, as I knew they would be, sad. I have to turn away.

I always enjoy the times when a man is recovering. I stay near the hut as much as I can. (The kitchen garden gets well tended.) I like it when he's hurting too much for me to *really* get to know him so I can make up anything I want. I can pretend he's on my side and we're friends. Actually I pretend we're lovers. We're all starved for males here, though we don't talk about it.

The prisoners are always wary—flinching at every noise or fast move. At night they groan and cry out. I make sure it's quiet for them. My hut is set well back, away from the rest of the village. I do sing. I think a woman singing soothes them. Bathing helps, too. I bathe mine every few days. They always fall in love with me but it's not real love. Being cared for after all that torture, makes them grateful. Some call me an angel. Of course later on, on the terraces, they change their minds.

The general mostly seems to listen ... to the birds ... to the sheep and goats when they're brought in to be penned for the night. . . . (Mine are penned up at a neighbor's for the time being and my daughter sleeps at friend's.) I suspect he's trying to figure out where he is.

He doesn't talk but I haven't talked either. I like it that way. When he starts talking I'll have to face who he really is but for now I can daydream all I want. I pretend the war is over and here's my husband, come back to stay.

Sometimes it's right when the prisoners are getting better that they have the worst nightmares. This time I can't wake him up. I stir the fire so I can see, then I shake him hard, and harder, but I must have hurt him more. He thinks he's being tortured again. He lashes out at me. I shy away and bang my head against the stone fireplace. He won't stop fighting. I don't know what to do. Finally I lie over his shaking body and hug him. Hold him down.

Right away he stops yelling and puts his arms around me and I feel, yet again, the lack of my man. I even think, serves my husband right. (I'd not, ever before, even been tempted to lie down on top of a prisoner no matter how he was yelling, but this one is my choice.)

He runs his hands up and down my back, pulls me tight against him . . . as if I'm his salvation. I feel his erection. I forget . . . that he's a prisoner and I, his overseer—though he doesn't know that yet. Perhaps he thinks I'm his rescuer. (They often think that in the beginning and are surprised when I, wearing my pistol, bring them to the fields to work.) He kisses me. First my forehead and cheeks (I feel his scratchy unshaven jaw against mine) and, then desperately, he kisses my lips (as if only my kisses could save him from more torture). I let him. His breathing . . . mine also . . . is ragged. He trembles more than he'd done back when he was yelling. I do, too. He holds me against him by my buttocks. I let him. It's been so long since I'd slept with my husband—or anybody.

But then I think how all I know of this man I've made up myself in my daydreams. Maybe I don't even like him. I probably don't really want to do it. I'd be in big trouble if anything happened. And do I want yet another half-breed of the enemy roaming about? Do I want my daughter taken from me—and me, thrown out of my village?

I pull myself away. I begin to cry . . . out of fear of what *I* would do, not what *he'd* do. He lets me go right away, so fast I feel abandoned even though I'm the one that stopped it. I'm on my knees beside him but I turn my back so he won't see me cry. He's still not well, but he sits up, groaning—I suppose in pain, and puts his hand on my shoulder. I'm tempted to turn around and let myself get hugged. He keeps saying how sorry he is and how good I've been to him all this time and how it won't happen again. He seems to think it's all his fault. I know I had a part in it. I say, "I tried to calm you but you kept shouting. I couldn't wake you." That's my excuse but it's a lie. I wanted to be close to somebody male again.

I build up the fire, and we sit on the pad before it and talk for the first time and I like him—more and more. Before, it was just my made up person that I liked, but now I like the real man. That scares me.

He's the one, now and then, that reaches over to stir the fire or put on another log. I feel. . . . But of course, I picked him out on purpose to fall in love with. I hope he's not as nice a person as he seems.

He asks me where we are. I say I'm not allowed to tell, but there's a good view of Basin Mountain. I say that on purpose. I know he'll know. He asks, is he a prisoner? When I say, yes, he says he thought so. Then he thanks me for treating him so well all this time. He asks my name. We're not supposed to tell them, but I do. Mara. And I ask his. We're not supposed to ask that either. We're supposed to name them anything we feel like that's short and easy to remember. (Sometimes their names are peculiar and hard to pronounce. I call all mine Don. A name I don't care anything about.) He's Sebastian. He says again how sorry he is. How I don't have to worry, he'll never do any such thing again.

All of a sudden I'm worried about my freckles, my chopped off hair. . . . Do I have even one thing to wear that's remotely female? And my calloused hands! How can my touch feel gentle and womanly? Then I think: What am I doing? At my age? At *my* age!

I could have talked 'til dawn, but I'm feeling so strange. And I'm still shaky. I know I won't sleep, but I have to leave the firelight that flickers over his face, that sparkles in his eyes when he turns to look at me. Even with those old clothes I dressed him in, he has a kind of dignity. And when a sad man smiles . . . !

I have to think. I tell him we should sleep. Of course after I go to bed I neither sleep nor think.

My room is large. There's a place for my loom. My bed is away from the fireplace on a kind of bench. It's behind the table. (When there are guests they have to sit on my bed to eat.) I'm far enough across the room to feel safely hidden from him but I can hear the rustling of his every move, his grunts and groans.

In the morning he seems much improved. He sits up. Stretches. I think to wrap the blanket around his shoulders but I don't dare get close. I don't even dare go see to the fire. He does it. Things have changed between us. When I hand him the breakfast gruel I don't look at him. Out of the corner of my eye I see him glance at me, as if to ask something. I eat at the table in the far corner by my bed. He eats on the floor by the fire. We don't speak. We didn't speak before either, but now it seems self-conscious. I'm in a hurry to leave. Besides, the turnips need putting away in the underground bins before the frost. I grab my hoe and go out without washing our bowls and without saying goodbye.

But I don't go up to our field. I stay close and work in the kitchen garden. I have this feeling that I have to protect him. What if the other women knew he was a general and thought he was too dangerous to have around?

I leave the hoe and get down on my hands and knees. Working like this has always helped me when I felt upset.

Then . . . here he is, working beside me. I hadn't heard him coming. Again, we don't talk, but this time the silence is companionable. My birds warble. The donkey watches from over the fence. The sun warms us.

When we go in for lunch, and he's walking beside me, I see he's a smaller man than I expected—not much taller than I am. But it's too late now, I like him even so.

Inside, I see he's washed the bowls and put them on the shelf. Rolled the sleeping pad and stood it against the wall. He's straightened out my bench-bed, too. When . . . *when!* has anyone ever, ever, ever done such things for me? I have to turn around and go right back outside. I wish there was a place where I could be alone. But there's nothing to do out there except take a few big breaths and go back in.

I fix him bread and lard, but I can't eat. Thank goodness he doesn't say anything or look at me.

The minute I take him to work on the terrace, my daughter will have to come back. That's the rule. You can't hide things from children. They see right through you. I don't want to take him to the fields but if the weather turns too cold the turnips will rot.

I'll go up by myself. I can't do much alone but I'd get some done. I have to get away and try to forget what I've started. I leave without any lunch. I'll nibble outer cabbage-leaves. (The main part of the cabbages have to go to the army.)

All the fields are narrow terraces, one on top of the other. Mine is the highest of those still used. It's a hard climb. My general will have to be in fairly good shape just to get up here.

Always, once I get there, I turn around and waste more time than I should, looking at the view. I feel renewed just looking. You can see all the way to headquarters. Farther on, you can see the flashes of the mortars, though you can only hear them when the wind is right.

When you look in the opposite direction, up to the snowy peaks, past the old, unused terraces, abandoned when the men left for the war, there's an old castle so high you can just make it out. There are lights up there. They say it's haunted. Once a woman went up. They found her at the bottom of the cliff, shot five times.

When I finally let myself climb down from my field, I'm so tired I don't think I could blush if I wanted to. I stop where my daughter is staying before I come to my own hut. She rushes into my arms shouting, "When can I come back? What's he like? Is he going to be a good one?" I say, "Soon as he's a little better," and, "I'm not sure if he's a good one yet."

He's asleep when I get back. I don't see anything changed this time, but I'll bet he's been snooping. Things don't look quite right but I couldn't say why. I sit down over tea, to rest for a while and look at him. He's sleeping as though exhausted still, curled up and covered with the blanket. I'll not wake him by stirring the fire. I'll use the propane burner to heat the grease to fry the finches.

It's the smell of frying birds that wakes him. I lay two places at the table. He gets up, is about to sit down, then hesitates, asks, "Is it allowed?"

Of course it's not, but I say, "Yes." And then I realize I can't do it when my daughter comes back. "That is, until my daughter comes."

"You have a daughter."

I say, "And a husband."

I see him hesitate with half a bird in his mouth. He chews more slowly, thinking.

I tell him that when I take him out to the field, I'll have to bring my pistol or else the women will wonder. He says he understands.

I always like nights in front of the fire, making things or repairing things. That little goats-wool cap of his won't be much help up here. I start on a wide brimmed hat.

That night it happens again—he yells, but this time I manage to wake him without too much trouble. I hold him as he calms down. Then he sits up beside me and we hold each other. This time it's companionable. At first. By now we know each other better. He says, "It's going to be all right." But then he's kissing me again. Suddenly he stops. And says it, too. "Stop me!"

But I don't want to. I don't care what happens.

We fall asleep in each other's arms, warm by the fire. I'm thinking, he's right, from now on, everything is going to be fine.

I wake when he brings me tea the next morning. I can tell it's late. I pop up. "I haven't time for tea. Did my daughter come by?"

"I told her you were tired. She looked in at you. She wanted to wake you but I told her not to. I'm coming to help you. You were so exhausted yesterday."

"But when my daughter sees you on the terrace she'll have to come back home."

"I want to help. Isn't that what I'm for?"

My cheeks are scratched from his needing a shave. I wonder if it'll show and the women will all know what happened.

"I have to take my pistol."

"I know."

He still limps, (they had torn out toenails), but he climbs to my terrace with no trouble. At the top we do what I always do, look down on the village and the switchbacks and then headquarters, all laid out as if a map.

Below us, here and there, prisoners and women work on the terraces. One woman, one prisoner, one donkey to a terrace. Here and there a child helps out.

Then we turn around and look up. Above, on the old deserted terraces, are the sheep, and above them, on the ground too steep even for terraces, are the goats. I wave to my daughter. She's hardly more than a red dot. She waves back like crazy, even does a little dance. She knows a man on our terrace means she can come home.

He says, "Is that High Peak outpost? I've not seen it before. Looks to be a day's climb."

"I suppose. We don't go there. There's lights up there at night."

He looks at it as if thinking about it, as if judging the trail up, then turns and looks down one more time as if memorizing everything, and then we get to work.

That night I'm happy even with my daughter here. She talks and he talks back. She even asks him what they call him. First he says, "I told you, Sebastian." She says, "No, I mean when you were little, like they call me Sisi though my name is Simone." He says, "Basti."

Sisi says, "I knew it!" though how could she?

I love to see a sad man throw back his head and laugh.

She says, "Shouldn't you sleep outside by the door like you're supposed to?"

He says, "You're right," and gets the blanket and gets

ready to go out, but she starts to cry. "I didn't mean you should do it. I want you to be warm in here with us."

"We'll give him the bench," I say before she has a chance to say how nice and warm she'll be sleeping with us both. Is she too young to know we shouldn't?

He slaughters a sheep for us. We leave parts to simmer as we go up to the field. Sisi goes on, up higher with the goats. Of course we have to share the mutton. You can't butcher a sheep and not have everybody know about it. That night we give Sebastian the head in broth, all to himself. I tell Sisi not to tell anybody he got the best part.

I like to see a strong man struggling with the plough in a way I couldn't do. He's good at it, too. He works like a peasant. I ask him how he knows . . . he, a general . . . all the things an ordinary man would know, plowing, butchering, and such. He says he *is* an ordinary man. He says he became a general in the field.

He still has nightmares. I think he was tortured more than the men I usually have. Since he's a general, he probably knew things. When he yells, I rush to the bench to wake him. Sisi starts to cry. She only stops when I tell her to come and help me comfort him.

Now and then Sebastian and I find a moment to ourselves. Once we went into the donkey shed.

Cold weather is settling in. I keep him in with us though it's not allowed. But most of my other men didn't last through the winter. I'm weaving in the evenings and piecing out the wool for trousers and jackets for all of us. We're quiet and cozy. It's Sisi who talks and asks. I find out things about him I never would have learned without her.

"Do you have a sister? You're old. Is your mama alive? Is she too old, too? Do you miss your sister and your ma? Have you ever gotten shot? Did it hurt? Did you ever almost cut your thumb off? I did. Did you ever throw up? I did. Did you ever cough so hard you turned yourself inside out? Did you have a picnic on your birthday? Do you like my mom?"

(It's yes to all these.)

When have I ever been this happy?

The next sunny day he says to bring a picnic and not tell Sisi. We pack bread and lamb fat and a blanket. There's no place to hide near the terraces. We go higher, up into the trees and boulders but far from where the goats are browsing. He spreads the blanket for me.

His beard has grown. It's soft against my cheek. It's coming in mostly white though his hair is only partly grey. I say, "I love you," but I know it won't do any good. All he thinks about is war.

After, he hides the blanket under a thorn bush. I'm happy, thinking, it's for another time. But it isn't.

Well, that's that, then. My pistol's gone, too. I don't want to ever bother with another prisoner. I'll do the work myself.

Not only that, eight of our prisoners went with him. Thank goodness nobody knows it's my general did that. Nobody even knew he was a general.

I should have guessed. Before he left he slaughtered two goats for us. Hid the meat so it looked as if he'd only killed one so we only had to give a part of one to the neighbors.

I have a feeling the men went up to that old castle. I remember how he looked at it and thought about it.

I climb to where the snow begins and look for tracks. I ask Sisi to tell me if she sees any. I tell her they might be from Basti and we need to know where he is and if he's all right. She doesn't act like herself at all now that he's gone. I hear her crying at night. She doesn't want me to know so I pretend I don't. She curls up beside me but I lie flat on my back and look up, stiff with fear.

I'm pregnant. Not a one of our men has been back here for months. Everybody will notice soon.

Every night I look at the lights shining from the castle.

They look warm and inviting. I have such yearning. But I don't even know if Sebastian is up there.

I don't tell Sisi what I'm planning. I pack when I'm supposed to be on the terrace. I pick her up on my way. Our goats follow.

Sisi is frightened. I can tell because she doesn't ask any questions. Not only that, she doesn't talk at all. We go fast. The goats love this. The steeper it gets the more they like it.

I thought we'd be there by evening. The trail is washed away in so many spots—that makes it take longer. We huddle down for the night. Sisi says right out, she wants to go home.

"Don't you want to see Basti?"

"Not this much."

"Of course you do."

"How do you know he's there?"

Now I'm the one ready to cry. I say, "I don't know what to do."

"It's all right, Ma." She hugs me. "You don't need him, you have me." Then she says what I always tell her. "You'll feel better in the morning."

She falls asleep right away, but I don't. She's right, I don't know where Sebastian is. If I were a general and had eight men with me I'd try to get back to my own army. I wouldn't climb up to the castle. What good would that do?

From here, so close, you can see long strings of lights up there. They're so intriguing. They look warm.

But next morning we look up at the grey cliff, streaked with breaks and lengthwise cracks, stained as if etched with black. The castle is made of the same grey rock it sits on. Now that we're this close and it's daylight, I can see the castle isn't a castle at all, but a fort with redoubts every hundred yards or so. It doesn't look as inviting as at night. And it does look haunted. Who would want to be here? What land is it protecting except land too steep to use?

167

There's no way to get up there except from around the back. I'm starting to feel as Sisi feels. Why am I doing this? And what about that woman that got shot?

We eat the rest of our food. We all—the whole herd of us—take off, skirting the cliff below the fort.

Sisi says, "Is it the enemy's? Is Basti up there because he's an enemy?"

"Maybe."

"He's not *my* enemy."

"Nor mine."

"I like enemies."

Of course those are the only men she's ever known.

We keep circling. We find a sort of stairway. Actually, the goats find it. If they'd not been here we wouldn't have noticed it. It's almost too steep for a human being. There are chains along the sides to help pull yourself up by. It winds in and out of cracks in the cliff until we're finally right up against the fort.

A shot hits the dirt in front of us the minute we step out from behind the rocks. Somebody calls down from the wall. "Who goes there?"

"A woman and a little girl. We don't know the password."

"Approach so I can see you."

We do. "It's Mara and Simone, come looking for General Sebastian."

"Climb to the left and enter through the gap."

There's a ramshackle wooden door. It's so beat up we probably could have crawled under it. The man who opens it is wrinkled and white haired and bent. He's an old-age kind of thin. He's wearing an officer's uniform of the enemy. The elbows and knees are completely worn through, threads hang from the wrists. He has a dozen medals on his chest along with food stains. He points an old rusty rifle at us as we come in, but he puts it down so as to check us for weapons. Even Sisi, top to bottom. When I object he says it's regulations. With me he spends more time than is necessary on my stomach. I've been wearing loose clothes down in the village, but they don't hide anything from him. He says, "You're pregnant."

"This is the general's baby."

"The general does as he wishes."

Sisi gives a little yelp of surprise.

The old man picks up the rifle and holds it, again as if to shoot us if we make a false move. "Come."

We go in, goats and all, past another rickety, rotting door.

There's no "inside" to the place—just one side of the wall and the other. There's the side where there's nothing but cliffs, and this side, rocky and full of rubble. It's the same as headquarters, just as dirty and full of garbage—smells just as bad, except headquarters is flat.

There are men all over, all of them ragged and thin and old. Most are squatting over smoky fires. (I wonder how long our goats will last.) Those who are walking are hobbling over the rubble. Some use their rifles as canes. At first I think they're all the enemy but then I see our uniforms are there, too. There's the yellow-brown goat's wool tams of their side and the navy blue caps of our side.

The old soldier puts us in a tent with a little heater. It has a wall of stones up to about three feet and then a canvas roof. I can just barely stand up at the center. There are two cots. I ask if we can have supper. The old man says it might be possible.

The minute we're alone Sisi says, "Why didn't you tell me you're having a baby. I thought you were just getting fat. I'm glad. I always wanted somebody else."

We wait. Nothing happens. Sisi says she knew coming here was a bad thing, and, "Why couldn't we stay down there and have the baby?"

"We can't. The women don't want an enemy's baby around."

Sisi puts her hands on my stomach. Just then the baby kicks. She yelps again. Says, "I love you," and gives my stomach a kiss.

Finally they bring us food—brought by another old

man very like the first. He brings outer cabbage-leaves and goat cheese. They have no better fare up here. Or maybe just not for us.

We wait again. It gets dark. No one brings us a light. There's nothing to do but try to sleep. Sisi and I cuddle up on one of the cots. Sisi falls asleep right away. I've had a hard time sleeping ever since I brought Sebastian in on my cart.

He comes in the middle of the night. Bringing a lamp.

Finally.

We hug. Or rather I hug. I surprise him with it. It feels like hugging a board. He's been too busy being a general. He sees . . . feels right away the shape I'm in. It takes a minute before he lets go—softens into a different kind of man, his arms around me, his lips against my neck. Finally we sit on the other cot. We whisper. Sisi still sleeps.

"Why are you here? You're not that old."

"Why are you?"

"I was looking for you."

"I'm going back. I'll pick up the rest of your prisoners on the way down. I'll bring the old men the battle they've been hoping for. I'll take you home on the way down."

"I can't go home like this. Why can't we go off together, someplace where there's no war? But which side will these old men be fighting for?"

"Their own side . . . a third side. A side to end all wars."

"End wars by war?"

"Remember these are their fathers. The men look up to them."

"You'll swarm down from the hills and attack our men from the rear?"

"We will."

"These old men are the ones who started the war in the first place."

He just grunts.

"You never had a real life either, did you?"

He grunts again.

"You think of nothing but war. Let's stop. Let's run away."

"We'll wipe out your terraces on the way down. They're so steep it won't take much. One landslide would sweep them all away. Since your hut is the highest, it will be wiped away, too."

"I wish you'd wipe away the whole valley. Cover the garbage with nice clean gravel. I'm so tired. If this baby is a boy. . . ."

The old men are eager to get to fighting. They're making sure all the old rifles are in good shape.

Everybody is busy. The whole place is changing. At the prospect of fighting again they're all standing straighter, doing exercises, push-ups and squats, marching around the area—as best they can over the rocks and rubble. Trumpets are sounding again. They're practicing the charge, though they're still sounding out a lot of wobbles and burbles.

They put Sisi and me in one of the redoubts. The stone walls make it colder and damper than the tents. We have a room to ourselves and one narrow window. Sebastian comes every night. We don't make love—I'm too uncomfortable and he's too tired, but he warms me in his arms. There's no doubt he needs somebody to hold him. He still wakes up yelling now and then, or sometimes has a long series of groans as he sleeps. I always think: Why don't we run away? but I don't say it.

Sisi comes in with us whenever Sebastian yells. It doesn't matter anymore. Besides, it's warmer for all of us.

And all this time he's looking even gaunter than before. The circles under his eyes, darker than ever. This doesn't make sense. The third side will make everything worse. It'll be more of a shambles than it already is. I think he thinks so, too.

One evening I say, "Please, please, please," hardly meaning to. And he says, "What?"

He thinks I mean something about myself, says, "I'll see to it that you're looked after."

"No, I mean you. What about you?"

But I'm worried about myself, too. What will happen when my time comes? Not one of these men will know how to help me. And I haven't taken very good care of myself. I'm cold all the time—even with Sebastian's arms around me. He finds me a sweater. Olive drab. One of his own I suppose, and it isn't as if he isn't cold himself. He looks worried all the time now. I wonder if he thinks none of his plans will work.

I run away to have the baby. I don't want anybody with me. I climb yet higher. I find a sheltered spot as far from everybody as I can. I hide behind rocks. (There aren't any trees up here.) I don't bring a lamp. I don't bring anything. I just go. Fast as I can. I feel dread. Fear. I don't know why. I don't even make sense to myself. These men are too old. Too warlike. It's as if, if the baby is a boy, they'll take it from me right away.

I thought it wouldn't take so long this second time, but by the time the baby finally comes, it's gotten dark. I can't see it. I think I did everything right. I wrap the baby in my cloak and in Sebastian's old sweater. I put it to my breast. The baby has a full head of hair. Our babies are usually bald. This is the enemy's child for sure.

In the morning I'm too worn out to try and get back. Besides, I don't want to go back. I don't feel like moving at all. Off and on I sleep. Later—much later—I hear people crunching and sliding on the scree. Panting. It's a hard climb. I'm in a little depression surrounded by boulders. I chose this spot specially. It's hidden and cozy.

I hear people calling out to each other, and calling for me, too. They're noisy. I'm glad I came up here and hid. I don't answer. I move even farther under the stones nearby. When it gets to be twilight, the people leave and I feel safer. I sleep again.

I wake when I hear tiny noises of pebbles trickling down.

I see a light, a tiny dim light wobbling back and forth. I'm even more frightened than I was earlier. It comes closer.

"Mara." He calls in a whisper. As though not wanting to scare me. But I *am* scared.

Then the little light flashes in my eyes, hesitates there, blinding me. And then it's lowered.

"Mara."

He doesn't touch me. He turns the light out and sits nearby looking up at the stars. He doesn't speak. Hardly moves. When he does start to talk it's as though to a frightened animal. First it's about looking at the stars and the new moon. Then, "I have food and blankets. I even have a little stove. I saw where you were when we came looking for you earlier. I thought to come back later alone. Can I light the stove?"

But I can't answer.

"I'll light the stove. You'll feel better after you have something to eat. It's been two days. You're starving."

It's a tiny stove but burns bright and bluish. He leans close, over a small pan. Again, as in front of our fireplace, I see the light flickering in his eyes but this time it shines blue and scary. But the soup smells good.

Just then the baby starts to cry. He holds still as though afraid to scare me. He even stops stirring the soup. I put the baby to breast. I refuse to look at him. I refuse to smell the soup.

When it's ready he squats beside me. "Just a sip or two. You'll feel better."

But I don't want to feel better. Why feel better when there's nothing to look forward to anyway?

It does smell good. He holds out the spoon. I sip. I go on sipping.

He treats me like a child. Says, "Good girl." I'm surprised he doesn't pat me on the head. I can see all this as if from over my own shoulder, but I can't react. I do feel better though.

After the soup he hands me tea. "I'd like to bring you back in the morning. Can you manage it?"

I can't nod.

He wraps me in blankets, me and the baby together, lies down and pulls me to him so his chest is my pillow. I have no will at all. I let him. He keeps on talking softly and as if it doesn't matter what he says, and it doesn't. I've done the same for Sisi when she was sick, and even for my donkey.

"You were good to me. You fed me. You held me. You. . . . And then you. . . . And then you. . . ." I don't listen to the words. I sleep.

When I wake, the baby's gone. I panic. I look to see if I've rolled on it or tossed it away in my sleep, but Sebastian has it. He's sitting nearby, cleaning it up with canteen water. It did need cleaning. He has white cloths to wrap it in. He came prepared for it and for me. He's talking to it as he talked to me—a lot of nothing. How many other babies has he fathered?

He looks up and smiles.

I don't smile back.

"I'll bring you tea in a minute. It's made." He wraps the baby in clean cloths and brings it to me. He props me up against blankets, my back against a rock, then brings tea and crackers. He crouches beside me and watches me eat.

After I nurse the baby, we start down. I don't want to go back but I don't know what else to do. I keep having the idea I must make decisions. But all I think is: *Think!* and then I don't do it.

He's not a big man, but he's wiry and strong. Sometimes he carries me and the baby—both his pack and me on his back. It's soothing—to have my arms around his neck and to feel the movement of being carried.

When we stop to rest and eat I say, "I won't go back."

"You need rest and care."

"I can't go back. Everybody knows."

"They know this is my boy."

"Boy?"

He gives me a odd look. And then an even odder one,

"What about Sisi?"

Sisi! Ever since I started up to hide and have the baby I've forgotten she existed.

"She came with us yesterday to help look for you. Didn't you hear her calling 'Ma'?"

Poor Sisi. I *did* hear. That must have been that lost goat sound.

Just in these three days things have changed at the fort. They're making black banners and hats with a zigzag of red. Like lightening and like blood. They're making flags that say, THE DEAD. And they do look dead. They could be dead. Why didn't I see that before? Bloodshot eyes, leathery skin, bony as skeletons. . . . They paint their faces a jaundiced yellow, though most of them look yellow anyway. They put charcoal around their already sunken eyes. If they're not really dead, they'll do for dead.

They'll advance in three waves. The first wave will pick up the other prisoners and take the pistols from their overseers. The second wave will fan out in a long line and loosen boulders to start the landslide. After the slide that destroys the terraces, the third wave will rush down, to and through headquarters, and hit our army from the back. They'll count on surprise and higher ground. They'll count on the fact that they're the dead.

If they're already dead they can't be killed over again . . . . Can they?

But killing each other—nothing new in that even if three sides instead of two.

I get better. I can talk again. I nod, smile, though it feels like I'm pretending.

Sebastian promises to run away with us as soon as this battle is over—off to some land where nobody knows him. That scares me more than if he hadn't said it. I know how it works with the last time for things. It means he's a dead man. If he survives to do as he promised. . . . I'll believe it when I see it.

The night before they're to go into battle he cries. Who

would have thought it, a general? I feel all the more that I don't want him to leave. I say, "Why not go right now? Cross the mountains. You want to. They can do this by themselves. If they really are the dead, they can do it."

Of course he thinks it all depends on him.

He's done for. I think he knows it.

We need more prisoners than usual to help rebuild the terraces. I build a little shed by my doorway almost as big as my donkey shed. I can house four. Several of us go down for more men.

Nothing has changed. Nobody seems to care anymore that my black-haired little boy is one of the enemy's. I suppose he's just one more soldier for our side. Nobody says a word about me coming back. They even help me repair my cottage. Sisi helps. I get better though I still have the sense I'm watching everything over my own left shoulder.

I don't think the dead were really the dead . . . or they died all over again. Or they were blown to bits. Maybe by their own rusty rifles. They weren't ghosts. I don't even wish they had been.

At headquarters we pick out new men. I see one that might be Sebastian—he wears a general's uniform. But I don't dare take anyone in as bad shape as this one. They wouldn't let me, anyway. I give him a drink of water. I wrap the old olive drab sweater around him. Whoever it is won't last long. It's a waste of a good sweater. One I especially liked for sentimental reasons.

JOSEPHINE

TOP OF LIST . . . ALWAYS at the top of list, rain or shine, day or night: Find Josephine. Nothing can be done until she's back here at the Old Folks Home where she belongs. Talent night she's our main attraction. We couldn't do much without her. She wobbles on her slack wire but she hasn't fallen yet. The ceiling is so high she can do the slack wire act in there in the living room though she has to watch out for the chandelier. She's not much higher than four or five feet up. When she sings she tinkles out the music on a toy xylophone. Once she brought her wind chimes down to the living room, put them in front of a fan and sang to that.

We pretend not to see how wobbly she is. Everybody else is worse. She's the only one with the courage to dance and sing no matter what. Or maybe it's not courage, just innocence.

Because of Josephine we often have townspeople visiting our performances. We don't know if they come to admire her or to laugh . . . at her and at us.

I'm the emcee, stage manager, entertainment committee. I'm less important than those who perform. I suppose I do have some poise, though I've been told I rock from foot to foot. Why would the Administrator pick a man like me for finding Josephine? Why pick somebody who has a limp?

No, I *am* the perfect person to send off to find her. Somebody she can have a good laugh at. She'll trip me and I'll be looking up from the sidewalk, right into her greenish-tan eyes. There she'll be, found at last, but she'll run off somewhere else before I can get up and hobble after her.

We live in a grand, though ancient mansion. It was the summer house of millionaires. They donated it to the town for us old people. The living room and dining room are often closed off—too hard to heat.

The breakfast room is the room everyone loves best and spends the most time in. It has windows on three sides with window seats under them. Five tables—enough for all of us. But I'm hardly ever in this room except to eat, nor is Josephine. Too many card games and too much bingo.

Josephine seldom comes out of her room except to eat and on show-and-tell night. (That's the only time we open the living room and let the heat come up.) Or she comes out to run away. She's *always* lost. If not right now, then she would be in another minute.

I wish I wouldn't have to be the one to find her. For the sake of the doing of a good deed, I do it.

She often says, "If not for *you* finding me, I'd not bother getting lost in the first place." I know that's true. When I find her (or should I say, when she lets herself be found) there's such a look of . . . well, it's complicated, disdain, but if that were all I wouldn't do it. There's relief, too. You'd think I'd find finding her worth it for that look, and I might if it wasn't for my arthritis. I've been using a cane lately. (Josephine gets lost in any kind of weather. Thank God tonight it's clear.)

You'd think by now the people in the neighborhood would bring her back when she strays, but they don't. They're afraid of her. Her hair is wild, the look in her eyes is wild and she makes nasty comments on their noses. She doesn't dress like anybody else. So many scarves you can't tell if she has a dress on under them or not. That must unnerve them. And the dress, which *is* under them, is more like a scarf than a dress. Everything she wears is like that, and it's always pinkish or pumpkin colored or baby blue. She always wears big dangly glittery earrings.

I step out on the porch. I admire the night for a few minutes as I always do. I hobble down the front steps. Our mansion has a few acres around it and trees so you can think yourself in the country, but no sooner out the gate and you're in town.

Sometimes I think Josephine is hiding just around the corner, watching me try to find her right from the start. Probably wondering which direction I'll look in first. Loving how my shirt tail's out, my belt unbuckled still. (I came straight from my bed.) Loving, especially, my big sigh.

I smooth at my mustache. I had no time to wax it and it's getting in my mouth. I can feel it's as draggled as the rest of me.

First I check the bushes on each side of the stairs to see if she's crouching there. She can hold as still as a frightened fawn.

I always bow when I find her. I do that because noblesse oblige. I wear my old boater just so I can take it off to Josephine. If ever she can be found smiling (that little I've-got-you-now smile) it's because of me.

I limp off, one helpless person in search of another equally inept.

Poor Josephine, here she is, in town somewhere, but I know yearning to be in a forest instead. She often says so.

Once a young person came knocking on our door asking for Great Aunt Josephine. (Just like Josephine, her eyebrows were so much the same color as her freckles they might as well not have been there.) Our Administrator lied. He said, nobody here by that name. She said she had papers. But he said the papers must be wrong and he could prove it with other papers. I suspect the Administrator is in love with Josephine.

The others here call the Administrator fuddy-duddy and fussbudget behind his back, but they don't expect that sort of talk from me. I call him Administrator. (I'm sure they call *me* fuddy-duddy and worse behind *my* back.)

Left, right or straight-ahead? It hardly matters. Sometimes she leaves me a sign, a little piece of unraveling rosy fabric from one of her scarves or a plastic flower stolen from the dining room tables, but no sign here now that I can see. I go out the gate, cross the street and down the hill. For no reason. I wish I could see more stars, but then I grew up in town. This is what I'm used to.

I whistle so Josephine can keep track of me.

I think I love her . . . or I must. At least in some way, else why do this practically every day? Every night? And with only a modicum of complaining? (And that, only to myself.) I think she cares for me, too. She's used to me, at least, and wants to torment me. That could be love.

Since I can first remember anything at all I've been in love. As if love came with consciousness itself. I fall in love all the time—always unrequited. I know there's something wrong with me, and I know that it shows, though I've no idea how people can see it as quickly as they seem to. But lots of people are prissy fuddy-duddies and manage to marry even so, while I've hardly even had friends. But I've stuck to my principles. I've been courageous in the face of misadventures. Even catastrophes. People can count on me. Josephine must have seen that in me from the start.

I suspect the Administrator knows only too well that I'm not the sort of man women fall in love with. I'm the safe one to send after her. Nothing will happen between Josephine and me. She practically told me as much herself. She said I was too polite. "Picky, picky, picky," she's said and more than once. I must admit I stick to my dignity as best I can.

As usual I'm not watching where I'm going. I'm looking up, wishing I could see more stars, but of course there's too many streetlights. I've so seldom been in a place where you can really see them. Here in town they seem unimportant. Even the moon, were it up, would seem unimportant. That's what I'm thinking when down I go.

At first it doesn't hurt, but then I try to get up.

"Josephine. I've hurt myself." I whisper it. How could Josephine help anybody?

I try again to get up. I *will* get up.

I can't. I have my belt. (I'm shocked to find it still unbuckled and my shirt tail still out. I try to be, if not elegant. . . . Who can be elegant with no money and with the bathroom down the hall and no lock on the door? People see you in all sorts of déshabille. Even so, I always try to be well-groomed. But I must be more addled than I thought.) I try coiling my belt about my leg. It's not going to help. I look around for my cane. I wonder if I should use it as a cane or a splint. I take my shirt off, twist it, and use it to tie my leg up tight.

I was cold to start with but now I'm colder. The way I'm shaking, I may be in shock. I lie back. I tell myself, have a bit of a rest. Maybe the pain will lessen in a few minutes.

No way to keep any dignity now. Josephine will come to laugh. I am prissy, and a fuddy-duddy, but I'm not a coward. I follow wherever Josephine leads. Once into the river. I had found her but she slipped out of my grip as we crossed the bridge and jumped in. I jumped in too. She knew I would. She can't swim even the little bit that I can. We were swept downstream half a mile before I managed to get us out. I had my arm around her. Even as I was busy trying to keep our heads above water, I thought: I have my arm around Josephine!

Neither of us told anybody though I suspect the Administrator had to be aware that we came back soaking wet. We left smudges all across the hall and up the back stairs. Did Josephine care that I spent my middle of the night cleaning up the worst of it as best I could? Of course she didn't, she thinks I'm much too neat and prim about unimportant things like a little bit of water—except there was also mud.

I see her. I *think* I see her. She's above me, poised on a tree branch as though about to do her slack wire act. It's shadowy up there, the light from the streetlight doesn't reach. But perhaps it's just a plastic bag. Josephine, what with all those scarves, has that same flimsy, maybe-there, maybe-not-there look all the time.

I wait, shaking. Wondering, still, whether it's better to use my cane as splint or cane. I try again to get up. I can't. I shout at myself, *"Do it!"* I push myself up on one knee. *"Doooo it!"* But I can't.

Then I hear Josephine whisper, "Don't do it," right in my ear, her hand on my shoulder exactly as lightly as you'd think her touch would be. She has her malicious grin but she's already found a splint. A discarded slat of some sort. She takes off some of her scarves. She puts one around me. It must be silk. (Of course silk, Josephine would never have anything but silk.) I feel how warming it is right away. Her hands are warm, too. And she has the touch—the healing touch. She takes my shirt and belt from around my leg and binds it to the slat with scarves. Then she puts her arms around me and warms me with her own body. She says, "I love you," but then she adds, "loyal sycophant."

Every time I find her she calls me that, or "Flunky." Sometimes, *"My* good man," emphasis on the *my*. She always smiles that mocking smile and says, (and what a ridiculous thing to say) "I'll make you a blueberry pie, I'll cook up a half a dozen escargots, *my* good man." They'd never let her anywhere near a stove or any kind of fire. It's another kind of torment just as saying, "I love you," is to torment me, too. Even her arms around me are meant to add to my misery.

My boater (ridiculous to wear such a hat in the middle of the night) is lying beside me, more out of shape than usual. It already was a little the worse for wear. (You can't get hats like this anymore, except maybe at a costume store. And I haven't any money anyway.) Had I found her as I usually do, I'd have bowed and removed it and held it over my heart, and Josephine would have smiled her little I'll-get-you-yet smile. I guess she has me where she wants me now.

We rest a bit and I am warmed and feel less pain. She strokes my forehead. She even smoothes my mustache away from my mouth. Here's her, Now-I've-got-you-smile, only now it's: Now-I've-*really*-got-you and she has a sly look of making plans. I suppose I'll have to do whatever she decides. But then I always do.

She helps me up. My leg, bound to the slat in silk, is as stiff as a cast. But I'll have to use my bad leg now. "I can't go far."

"It's not far."

Not far? What in the world could be not far? Especially to somebody with two bad legs.

There's a muddy rivulet flowing across the sidewalk near us. Josephine says, "This little trickle is the fountain of youth."

I can't help but laugh out loud. There's a faucet dripping somewhere. Maybe some lawn sprinkler has dribbled all the way down here where there aren't any lawns.

"You're thirsty," she says. "Drink. Lean and drink."

I am thirsty, but I won't drink this.

"All right then, if you won't be young and gay again, let's go."

She has put my boater back on my head for me. At a rakish angle of course. That's to tease me, too. Here I am shirtless, though wrapped in her scarf. Did she bother to help me back into my shirt? She lets it lie there. I don't have that many shirts. She must know that. Back at our mansion there's not much we can hide from each other. I've turned the collar, but one side is now as worn out as the other.

She helps me. Here she is, hardly coming up to my shoulder and yet strong enough to really support me.

Of course she's strong, how can you be a dancer and slack wire walker, tree climber without being strong? I've noticed before how muscled her legs are.

This is exactly what she's always wanted, I can see it in her eyes. Her mouth twitches. She can't hide her smile though she's trying.

We walk over my shirt and go. I'd much rather stay here and wait for help. I'd like to be carted off to the hospital. That would be a nice change. I'd be able to eat by myself. I'd be all cleaned up. Josephine could come visit. She wouldn't. She would. She'd like to see me in bed with maybe my leg in traction.

I haven't paid attention to where we've been going. I've been too concentrated on how to keep on than to notice where. Here we are in some alley I've not seen before.

I'd like at least to wait until the pain subsides, but Josephine pulls me on. "Come on, my own, you can rest in a minute."

I go where she wants me to as I've always done, but I'm feeling dizzy and nauseated. I know what that means, I'm going to faint if I don't sit down, and right away.

Next thing I know my own groaning wakes me. I stop as soon as I realize it's me making that racket. I'm crumpled up in the backseat of a roadster. Top down. I may be thin but even so I can't imagine how Josephine got me there. Here she is driving down the road, no lights. She's driving by the streetlights. I wonder how long I've been out of it. My leg is propped up on the door. My boater is on the floor. I'm covered with a dusty, moth-eaten army blanket.

The car seems as old as Josephine. Has she stolen it? If she has, why didn't she steal one that has working headlights?

I fade off and when I come to I'm groaning again. It's because the road is suddenly bumpy. We've gone beyond the streetlights. Josephine drives slowly, by the stars.

The road is little more than two ruts now, and soon the trees above us close off the stars. And Josephine is driving by instinct. Or perhaps the ruts force the car in the right direction.

This must be her forest. The one she's wished to be in all this time. But why didn't she come here long ago, by herself? Or did she need a sycophant? A watcher? As if her whole life means nothing without me to observe it?

We go on and on. I'm gasping at every bump and there's nothing but bumps. It's like being on a small boat in choppy seas. I'm actually feeling seasick.

Dawn is coming. I can see Josephine's windblown mop of hair in silhouette against the grayness. I see the glint of her dangly earrings.

I call out, "I'm going to be sick."

She stops the car and helps me lean over the side. She holds my forehead. She calls me, "My dear," but I'm too miserable to think anything about it.

As to my dignity, that she teases me about every day, there's none left. My vomit and my sweat are all over me.

"We're already there," she says. "We're home."

Home!

But we bounce on, and dawn keeps coming. Things are turning pink. We round a corner into a clearing, and there's a sudden breeze. We stop near a lake full of whitecaps—pink whitecaps. When Josephine stops the car I can hear the lapping. On one side of us there's a clapboard cottage in need of paint and on the other a tumbledown shed. Ahead of us a rickety dock slanting at a crazy angle.

I'm so sick and exhausted I don't want to move. I pull back when Josephine tries to help me out. She gives up and goes inside, screen door slamming (at first I think we're being shot at) and comes out in a few minutes (another rifle shot) with hot tea. It tastes odd, dusty and stale, but it helps right away. Powerful stuff. No doubt some Josephine-type secret herbs in it.

Now she helps me in. The shutters are closed so it's dim inside. Moth-eaten deer head on the wall, a half a dozen fishing rods crosswise on its antlers. Its eyes glitter with what little light there is.

Josephine plops me down on an overstuffed chair. Dust flies up and I sneeze. She props my bad leg on a footstool. Then she goes into another room and comes back with a white shirt. Seems brand-new. But then she sees how filthy I am, sidewalk dirt and vomit, tea stains. . . . She brings a basin of warm water and towels and soap. Cleans up my top half.

She says, "No wonder. . . ."

First I think, no wonder what? But then I know: I'm much too thin and my chest much too concave so of course no wonder. No wonder I'm nothing but a toady.

"I'm going to leave you here alone and go get groceries."

"Get me crutches."

I can see she won't. Why should she, now that she finally has me completely in her power?

"Please."

She looks away. At least she won't lie. There's always that about her. I appreciate it.

"I'll get night crawlers. If you want to fish right now, dig one up. You can drop a line at the end of the dock."

What a silly thing to say. Well, maybe not if she wants to tease me with suggesting things I can't possibly do.

"Watch out for snapping turtles."

Indeed.

She's off (she reaches to pat the neck of the deer head on her way out, then comes back and kisses him on the lips. Sawdust trickles out.) Here I am, sunk (too deep) in the chair. But clean—top half anyway—and with a new shirt.

I pull myself up, sneeze again from the dust, and prop myself up on the arm of the chair. Using my arms and my one good/bad leg I support myself over to a harder chair. The deer's eyes follow me like those in front-staring portraits always do. There's disapproval in its look.

If I tip this hard chair from one side to the other, I can make progress. Without Josephine's herbs I'd not be able to manage it without pain. It takes a long time. When I get to the closest window and open shutters, here's Josephine driving up. I notice now that the roadster used to be red.

I watch her bring in packages. She seems much more efficient than she normally is. Likely her confused look, and wandering away all the time was one more game.

I wonder where she's been, because the first thing she does is hang wind chimes in the doorway. They set to tinkling right away. Can't she do without that sound for half a minute—even here with ripplings and rustlings?

She doesn't pay attention to me but busies herself in the kitchen. There's not exactly running water but there's a pump next to the sink and every time Josephine needs water I hear lots of its creak-creaking. It sounds as if it's in more pain than I am. Josephine sings and hums. I've never heard her sound so happy. She brings me broth—store-bought broth, the kind we always have at the Home.

"There's real broth simmering on the stove," she says, "but it'll take a while."

She plops herself down in that overstuffed chair and puts her feet on the footstool she'd pushed over for me. She gives a big sigh just like the one I always sighed before I started off looking for her. Before I realize it (probably before she realizes it) she's asleep. She does look exhausted. After all she drove all night but I wish I'd stayed in the chair myself.

There's a screened-in porch. I wobble my chair out there and find a love seat just right for lying with my leg up on the arm. I fall asleep almost as fast as Josephine did. I dream a sick dream of being, not only a toady but a toad in fact, and of herbs that keep me helpless. In the dream I try to wrestle myself out of my own torpor. I fight to wake up and find myself fighting with the wicker back of the love seat, and then I'm on the floor fighting the floor, and then Josephine is beside me and I'm fighting her.

She slaps me, hard, on each cheek. It feels good because it wakes me out of my bad dream. How did she know to do that? Could she ever have been a nurse?

She sits on the floor beside me and pulls me across her lap, calls me, my dear, again.

I lie in her arms, poplars rustling, waves rustling. . . . There's a bird chirping right outside. I hear it all as if clearer than I've ever heard anything. I feel Josephine has me just where she wants me but I'm where I want to be, too.

After a while she puts a cushion under my head, goes and gets me more of that same dusty tea. She helps me back to the soft chair with the footstool and brings me broth that was on the stove all this time. In these few hours it has turned into real homemade broth with cloudy ribbons in it and little flecks of something or other. I've no idea what.

There's one other room, a little bedroom with a sagging iron bed. The white paint from the iron is chipping and lies all over the bed and floor. Josephine brushes it off and puts me to bed there. It has a lumpy, sagging mattress but I fall asleep instantly. I feel drugged, but I'm glad I am.

In the morning I wake to thumping and bumping and then something falling part way down stairs. Turns out there's an attic and there was an old desk chair on castors up there. She's carried it down the steep stairway, castors dropping off and down first. I don't think I could have done that even without a broken leg. She rolls it next to the bed, helps me on it, and pushes me out to the kitchen.

She has opened all the shutters. With the morning sun pouring in you can see the dust rising. You can even see our footprints across the floor. But Josephine doesn't clean up, instead (and it actually comes true, just as she said), she bakes me a pie. Not blueberry but mulberry. She's already been out picking things. For supper we have fiddleheads cooked in butter and fried puffball steaks.

I eat, dressed in another clean white shirt. It smells of having been hung on the line in the sun.

In the evening she rolls me out on the rickety dock away from under the trees so we can see the stars. My God, stars so dazzling and dizzying. . . . It looks as if any minute you'll fall right off the earth into them. She knows them all: Cassiopeia's Chair, Betelgeuse, Aldeberon, the Teapot, the Swan. . . .

Next morning she pushes me out on the porch so I can watch her as she rows herself out in the old flat-bottom boat. She catches a sunfish and a pike.

That evening we sit on the porch and listen to the birds settling down for the night. We watch the sun setting over the lake. First comes the wishing star and then more. Here on the porch, complete stillness, but all sorts of rackets going on outside, rustlings and tweetings, peepers peeping, bullfrogs karumphing.

Days pass like this. Soon I'm well enough to take little walks.

She hasn't been teasing me lately. Or, rather, her teasing is more playful. Even her warnings make me laugh. ("Watch out for the bears." "Watch out for rattlesnakes." "Watch out for roots that trip." "Watch out for ground-hornet's nests." "Watch out, watch out, watch out.") Then she'll put my dilapidated boater on my head, always at a rakish angle. "And don't step on any wild strawberries." I'm beginning to love a life like this. I'd like to learn to drop a worm into the water. How hard could that be? I'd like to pick gooseberries. First though, I'll dust this place. Josephine isn't going to do it. She doesn't seem to notice. I'm the one sneezing all the time.

I notice she has her parasol here, just in case of a slack wire. It suddenly appeared, crosswise on the antlers along with the fishing poles. It reminds me how much I miss Josephine's act. It's nice seeing birds perching on her head and feral cats coming when she calls but not as nice as that balancing act of hers.

We have our rituals: our cleaning of the lamp chimneys, our lamp lighting, our last cup of tea before bed, Josephine patting the neck of the deer head and giving it a goodnight kiss, sawdust dripping out every time.

My leg is better when the Administrator finds us. I'm able to hobble with my cane almost as well as usual. I've cleaned up. I've fished and picked berries. I've chopped wood and gathered kindling. We've been out with a flashlight and caught frogs for frogs legs.

By now we're so used to our wind and water sounds, our wind chimes, our screeching pump, that we hear him right away and from a long ways off. We look at each other over our lunch of crawdads and miner's lettuce. There's a sudden panic. We see it in each other's eyes. We're like children, caught in an act of mischief. Of course at first we don't know it's the Administrator. What we know is, this can't be good. Then, through the trees, we see the big black car the Administrator always drives.

I say, "Where?"

She says, "Follow me."

But I change my mind. I say, "No, we're grown-ups."

I've taken my usual role. Exactly what Josephine doesn't like about me the most.

"*You* may be," she says and is gone.

He comes alone. Black suit, striped tie and all—even way out here in the woods. He has a pistol in his belt. I can't imagine why, what with two (probably more addled than we think we are) old people.

I step out to meet him. *Bang!* goes the screen door. (I'm usually good at remembering to be careful.) I hold out my hand but he ignores it. "Well, well," he says. "Well, well, well." He looks all around: our shed, our paint-peeling cottage, our rickety dock. He can't stop saying, "Well."

Then we hear singing—raspy, wobbly, old lady singing. We look up and there's Josephine. Talk about not being a grown-up! She's dancing . . . I can't believe it, first across the cottage roof, holding her pink parasol for balance. Then . . . I can't believe it even more. My God, she's stepping out on the wire where electricity used to come into the house long ago when the electric bill was paid for. She's in no hurry. She turns, scarves twisting, goes back and forth, gives a little jump. We're mesmerized—as we always are when she does her act. After a minute or two of this, she goes off along the wire, and when a good tree comes along with nice straight branches, she hops out on those and then over to another tree and another. A scarf floats down. We lose sight of her after that.

If he takes me away, what will happen to Josephine? She won't stay here without me. She'll come back to the Home of her own accord. Is that what he's counting on?

I surmise . . . many surmises I had not surmised before. I couldn't stand the Home if Josephine wasn't there. She and I . . . once I really think about it, we both love being outside day or night in any weather. I didn't realize it but I loved chasing after her. It was our excuse for a little bit of freedom and adventure. I loved the responsibility and Josephine loved the misbehavior.

The Administrator looks at me in such rage! As if it's all my fault, *all* of it.

He shouts warnings and her name, and, "You'd better this or that, or else this, that, and the other." And then he shoots in the air.

I say, "You can't scare her. She doesn't scare," so he turns and points the pistol at me.

"Maybe I can scare *you*."

"Maybe."

He shoots in the air again. "Take me to her."

"No."

I couldn't anyway. God knows what hiding places Josephine has out there in her woods, and I don't know a single one.

He makes a barking sound then turns and shoots out our front window. I hear something fall inside. From the sound of it, bull's-eye. The deer head has gone down. I can't say I'm sorry. That deer head never did approve of me.

He puts the pistol down at his feet. I think to grab it. I could run . . . hobble. . . . Perhaps I can run faster than I think. Throw the pistol in the lake. But as usual I deliberate too long. He takes handcuffs out of his pocket, puts one cuff on my wrist and looks around for someplace good and solid to handcuff me to. There's no place. Finally he handcuffs me to the pipe that takes the water from the well in to the kitchen pump.

"At least *you're* not going anywhere."

He reloads and off he goes, following the wires, but first he shoots one more shot—at our jay. Misses. (That jay perched on Josephine's head almost every time we left the cottage.)

I fear for her, but I fear for him, too.

I try to squeeze out of the cuff until my wrist is raw. I move the cuff up and down the pipe.

And then, thump, here is Josephine, right beside me, dropped from the roof. She gives me such a smile! As if she'd heard the shots and thought to find me lying dead and yet here I am alive. "Thank, thank, God, God, God, God!" she says. She throws her arms around me and kisses me hard right on the lips. This time there's no irony in it.

She didn't have to come back. She could have stayed lost in the woods. I'll bet she has dozens of hiding places. I wouldn't be surprised if she didn't nest in the trees as chimpanzees do. I wouldn't be surprised if she didn't eat all sorts of leaves. We've already dined on nettles.

She gets a wrench from the kitchen and twists at the joint where the pipe enters the cottage. It's so rusty it won't move, but it does break and she slides the cuff off the end and I'm free.

She says, "Nobody knows he's here." There's that sly look again.

"Are you sure?"

"Why else would he come alone? And with a pistol? He wants me. You he'll kill and throw in the lake."

Just what I was thinking to do with him.

"He used to come to me at night until I started running away."

I'm shocked. Except. . . . Well, *maybe*, but it could be as ridiculous as that filthy fountain of youth.

"This is the perfect place for him. He'll tie me to the bed and come here every weekend. Feed me nothing but oatmeal. I know him."

Oatmeal—that part I know is true. It's our usual breakfast at the Home.

"I couldn't tell about it back there. Everybody thought I was too addled. They'd never believe me."

That's true, too. Even I don't know what to believe.

We hear shots close by. And then a squawk. Might be one of our ravens that we've been putting food out for. (I know it's only a raven, but it makes me angry. I may not be able to be as impartial as I wish to be.) Another shot, then lots of squawks. They're defending their own. I've a good mind to head off in that direction and help them.

Josephine must see it on my face. She says, "Go." I go. Weaponless except for my cane. Off into the woods with no sense of direction except raven calls. Like it or not I will be . . . I *am* her hero.

I tramp on mayapples and wild strawberry plants, mushrooms (toadstools I suppose), pass by a puffball and think, must remember where it is. The ravens stop. I stop. I listen. Without the ravens I have no direction to go in.

Yet I go on, more slowly now, listening between each step. I come upon a hut of leaves and branches, floor covered with a bed of ferns.

But why isn't anything making any noise? Why not even the ravens? There's just a stirring of leaves and the easygoing lapping of waves somewhere over on my left.

Then I hear him crashing towards me. I hunker down and wait and wonder what to do with no weapon except a cane. I think maybe crook it round his neck or trip him. . . . I think how he's a much bigger man than I am. Younger, too.

Instead of him I see a doe leap past. I hear a shot from right behind her. I'm thinking this is not a doe. Her mate was mounted on the wall and now lies on the floor. That deer head has looked at me with such suspicion all this time. I don't know where these thoughts come from. I know that can't be true. But then I see the glint of gold. Is the doe really wearing a long dangly earring or is it a trick of sun rays coming through the leaves in little spots of light? Did she wink? Or, rather, blink at me as she dashed by?

After the doe, here he comes. I no longer wonder if I should do this or that. I grab his leg as he goes by. I make him miss his second shot. How dare he! How dare, and even if the doe isn't Josephine? How dare? And in our forest! I'm on top of him, fearless. There's one more shot. First I'm thinking: Missed me! Then I'm thinking: He did it to himself.

It seems to me Josephine somehow choreographed the whole thing on purpose. Sent me off, then risked her life for . . . I don't know what. Me I suppose.

By the time I find my way back to the cottage it's dark, but, as I enter the clearing, it's a dazzling, shiny dark with Josephine—my God!—above me, on the telephone wires again dancing to a background of the constellations, skirt and scarves billowing out, parasol. . . . Quite extraordinary. And dancing better than I ever saw her dance. It would have been a joy to everybody back at the Home. Alas that only I am here to see it.

"My love." I finally dare to say it. "My only, ever and always love."

She hears. She says, "I am your heart's desire."

Is that yet another joke or irony? But of course it's simply real and true. I answer, "Indeed." Indeed.

WISCON SPEECH

✿

I gave this speech on Memorial Day at WisCon (the world's only feminist science fiction convention) in 2003. I was, besides being petrified, pleased and flattered to be the guest of honor, and especially so since this is my all-time favorite conference. It's the funniest and "silliest" (mostly they laugh at themselves) conference I've ever been to. At the auction they got down to auctioning off the piece of gum the auctioneer had been chewing . . .

✿

THIS IS MY FAVORITE convention. No other like it. It's the funniest.

These days I feel I should do a political speech. Or ecological speech, but I can't do that. Maybe China [Mieville] will do it. This is all about me and some about writing.

(Sort of ad-libbed until here.)

I've heard three or four speeches here. I can't remember

exactly, but it seems like all those writers were good students. Well, now you'll hear about a bad student. All my life a bad student. And I hated writing most of all. It was too hard.

One reason I was such a bad student is that, as a kid, I went back and forth to and from France. For a while it was back and forth every other year. I was eight years old in France, nine and ten here, then eleven in France, twelve back here ... etc.

At the age of eight I was dumped into a two room country school where nobody talked English except me and my brother. I was not aware of learning French. I was not aware of not being understood. I think I just talked and gradually it must have become French. (My daughter saw the same thing when she took my eleven-year-old grandchild to Peru. There was a boy his age next door and they played together, one speaking Spanish and the other English. They didn't seem to be aware that they weren't speaking the same language.)

So, going back and forth like that, in school I was hopelessly confused. I can't, even still, spell much of anything. I remember the exact words that made me decide I couldn't learn (and so gave up): address/adresse, and syrup/sirop. I thought, well, if that's how you spell "address" then obviously I can't learn anything so why try. I quit. I think I was eleven. It was as if a curtain came down and I didn't bother anymore. I did manage to squeak through with C's and a few D's. In college I failed freshman English and had to take it over and almost failed again. (Did I say my dad was a professor of linguistics at University of Michigan?)

Now studying and researching are my favorite things to do ... after writing. I know that's true with most of you, too.

Now writing is my favorite *because* it's the hardest thing I know. That's why I love plots and stories. I love the skill it takes to get everything together. Don't tell anybody but I think short-story writing is harder than poetry. Even harder than sonnets.

In France my brother and I stayed about a year each time, and usually in different places, but always with the same Frenchwoman. My parents and little brothers stayed in Oxford, England, and later in Freiberg, Germany, so I and my brother were alone, but that Frenchwoman was a much better mother than my mother was. My mother visited now and then and watched her in action and learned how to be a good mother from watching her.

One year my brother and I lived in a chateau that had an indoor outhouse, a two-holer. Downstairs. That didn't matter because the Brittany maid emptied the chamber pots every morning. There was a large living room full of marble statues, but they couldn't use it through the winter because they couldn't heat it. The only heated parts of the house were the small dining room, (as opposed to the large one) a small play room for my brother and me, and the kitchen. They had little stoves that the maid carried from room to room.

At a different place we stayed (a small house), you went up a bank outside and peed into a hole that went down into a vat. When it was full they carried it out to spray on the fields.

I didn't pay any attention in school but I did read a lot. *Tarzan* and *John Carter of Mars*, but especially Zane Gray and Will James. My parents and brothers would go off on the weekend but I'd stay home to read. I didn't read any "girl" books. I have three brothers and I always wanted to be a boy. (There was no doubt in my family which sex was the important one.)

I wasn't brought up as a girl, I was brought up as a defective boy.

I wouldn't have stooped to reading any book like *Little Women*. (All that was just as I was growing up. Not now. I've changed.)

But I was freer than my brothers because I didn't matter. Boys had three choices. They could become lawyers, doctors, or professors. (So my musician brother is the black sheep.) But it didn't matter what *I* did.

Writing my western novel, *Ledoyt*, I was having fun in several ways. I could go back to being a cowboy and I could be a man. (Like Flaubert said of *Madame Bovary*: Ledroit, c'est moi.) And I could draw for it exactly as I drew when I was in high school.

I hated anything to do with writing until I met science fiction people though my husband, Ed Emsh. (Freshman English ((and spelling)) had scared me off.) The science fiction writers talked about writing as if it could be learned and as if a normal human being could do it. Through Ed I got to know (and love) the sf world and wanted to join it. I began to sell stories right away—first to the pulpiest of the pulps. Later on I took classes at the New School with Anatole Broyard and Kay Boyle, but I learned the most from the class with the poet Kenneth Koch.

I've only been blocked when I've learned a lot. After my class with Kenneth Koch, I couldn't write for six months. I had learned so much I had to take time to absorb it. And yet I couldn't tell anybody what I'd learned. I tried even right after the class. What you learn is a secret. It's an experience you have to go through.

I also learned a lot from the various Milford science fiction workshops. And especially from Damon Knight.

I've been doing a lot of war stories lately. I want to give my credentials. Just as I started college, the men started being drafted. We'd look in the newspaper everyday to see which of our professors had been called up for World War II. Pretty soon most of the men were gone. (They were either in Canada, or 4F, or in jail for conscientious objecting, or in the war. My husband and my brothers went, though later my husband marched against the Vietnam War.) Though I was and am, more or less, a pacifist, I wanted to see what was going on. I wanted to experience what my generation was experiencing so I joined the Red Cross.

I spoke French so they sent me to Italy. I handed out

coffee and doughnuts, ran a club, and recruited girls for dances . . . *and* supervised a little library of paperbacks. (We weren't supposed to worry if they were stolen.) (That's when paperbacks first came out.)

By the time I sailed into Naples on a troopship, the war had *just* ended. I saw a lot of devastation but no actual war. First I was stationed on the Isle of Capri at an R & R (rest and relaxation) place. I can't remember doing a single lick of work. I played pinochle with the guys and took groups hiking on the cliffs. Later I was stationed in Tarcento near the Yugoslavian boarder. In neither of these places did I wear my Red Cross uniform. I learned a lot about how gross *some* (not many) American soldiers could be with the Italians. I was cursed at and spit on by some of our guys when they thought I was Italian. They called me words I'd never heard then and have never heard since. On Capri four or five men would get together and push down the thick mud walls surrounding the houses just for the fun of it. In Tarcento I do remember working. I drove a truck. I loved doing that.

So I went first to music school, then to war, and then to art school, where I met Ed Emsh. Actually we met in front of a naked lady—in life class. After we married, we went off to France for a year and studied at the Beaux-Arts. In the summer we rode all around Europe on a motorcycle.

When we came back, Ed started out as an science fiction illustrator, but then went into abstract expressionist painting and experimental film making. We influenced each other. I went into more experimental writing and became part of what others called the new wave in science fiction. That was a long time ago. Now I call it the old wave.

Kafka is my favorite writer. I love most of his short stories, better than his novels. (Though I don't care for *all* the short stories. My favorites are "A Hunger Artist," "Josephine the Singer, or The Mouse Folk," and "A Report to an Academy," which I imitated in *Report to the Men's*

Club) I like Kafka because his stories resonate beyond the story. And I like that you can't quite put your finger on the meanings. It's more a feeling that it's telling you more than is on the page. I recently heard a writer on the radio say that stories should be like icebergs, most of them underwater.

I've done many a story without resonance. (All my early work in fact.) But I don't care much for those stories of mine.

The nicest thing that was ever said about my science fiction writing was by Jim Gunn. He wrote that my science fiction stories "estranged the everyday." That's what I like best about science fiction. You can make the everyday seem strange. You can see ordinary things with new eyes. Sometimes alien's eyes. You can write about the here and now and have the reader see us as odd. Which we are.

Since thinking about this speech I've been watching myself write more closely than I usually do. I see that "estranging the everyday" is often why I work on a story in the first place. (I have several beginnings hanging around that I never went on with because they were simply telling "the story" so why bother?) Also I think it's science fiction's best reason for being. I like the other stuff, too. Some of it I like a lot, just not as much.

I'm finding, in my new war stories, that I can make anti-war comments through science fiction in a way I wouldn't be able to if I couldn't place the stories in a sort of limbo. My story "Repository" (out in the July issue of *The Magazine of Fantasy & Science Fiction*) would have been impossible without a science fiction premise that had wiped out all the soldier's memories so they weren't sure what side they were on.

Also I don't like to write about a specific war or place or time. I prefer to universalize it. Put it in limbo and make it stand for all wars. Science fiction is perfect for that.

A lot of people like science fiction because they're fascinated with gadgets and inventions and odd doodads and all different kinds of aliens, and that's fun and takes a lot of imagining, but I prefer stories with few science fiction elements.

I may have been brainwashed in this—that is in having as few sf elements and as possible—by Damon Knight. I obey that rule of his, but not his other rule. This was that, if a story can be told in a non sf way, then do it that way. He forgot that if you want to be a science fiction/fantasy writer then everything goes into that mold.

I always break Damon's second rule, so I guess you guys can break both of them if you want to.

I also have a problem with those stories where strange things, not foreshadowed, keep popping up. If anything can happen at any time, where's the suspense? As Damon Knight wrote, it's like that old joke about waiting for the second shoe to drop. (Somebody living above somebody else is going to bed and takes of his shoe and drops it on the floor. Then he realizes he's made a big thump for the guy below him so he very carefully puts down the second shoe. Pretty soon the guy below him knocks on the door and says, "For God's sake drop the other shoe.") In my classes I always say: But be sure to drop the *first* shoe so the reader can be waiting for the second. First shoes are as important as second shoes. I consider writing to be dropping a lot of first shoes.

After Ed died my writing changed completely. And my reasons for doing it. My children were scattered all over the place, my husband was dead. . . . I needed a family. I created kids, teenagers, and a husband to live with. I lived in my two westerns, *Ledoyt* and *Leaping Man Hill,* in a way I never had lived in my writing before. At that time those characters were much more real to me than my friends. I didn't go anywhere. I just wrote.

Another big change in my life back then pertains to *Ledoyt, Leaping Man Hill,* and also *The Mount.* One of my daughters said something important to me right after Ed died. She said go and do something you never did before.

She couldn't come with me but she sent me to a ranch.

At first I kept telling her: But I don't like horses anymore. After I'd been there I kept saying: It's the lore I like. All the stuff those ranchers know. How they go out as if ships, with everything to repair *anything* tied on their saddles. And I had never lived on a farm/ranch before. I had *no idea.* And I guess by now I finally say I do like horses.

In my novel *Ledoyt* I went back to being twelve years old in all ways. I drew for *Ledoyt* exactly as I used to draw in my notebooks in junior high. I loved the research so much I couldn't leave it out . . . so the recipes, and medical information of the times, etc., are in it. That was my first *real* novel. My earlier novel *Carmen Dog* is like a series of short stories, except, as in *The Perils of Pauline,* each short story gets her in more trouble at the end. I was so confused about writing a real novel; when writing *Ledoyt* I remember lining up all the scenes and sections in a long row across the floor trying to decide the order. But after *Ledoyt, Leaping Man Hill* just went zipping along. (Some people like the mess of *Ledoyt* better.)

Later at my summer place in California, I took several classes in prey-animal psychology, which actually were classes on the psychology of everything. About how we, being predators and having predators such as cats and dogs around us all the time, understand predators, but know very little about prey animals.

I used what I learned in this class for writing *Ledoyt,* but also especially in my novel *The Mount.* Especially the differences between prey and predator. I thought it would be fun to write about a prey riding on a predator instead of the other way around. Us, who can't smell and can't hear very well, and can only see straight out in front, being ridden by a creature who can see in a circle, and hear and smell better than we can.

Another fun thing about those classes was that only the ranchers came to them. People with lots of horses and lots of cows and big hats they never took off.

I don't think I ever would have written if I hadn't gotten

married. I came from a big, bouncy, noisy family. Always laughing and talking and arguing. (My dad was one who thought to argue was to love.) I was so lonely when I first got married with just the two of us, I didn't know what to do. I kept on with art work for a while, but after meeting the sf people through Ed, I wanted to join them.

I was a daydreamer, but what kid isn't? My parents let me alone. They didn't worry about my bad grades or whether my homework was done. They let me be. That wasn't just because I was a mere girl. They didn't worry about the boys either. They always thought we'd wise up one of these days all by ourselves and everybody did—but with me, it took a long, long time.

I didn't begin writing until I was thirty and had had my first child. (I had three, so I had to struggle to get any writing time at all. Most of the time I went around feeling as if I couldn't breathe.) I never really had writing time until my husband moved to California to teach at Cal Arts. For nine or so years we had a bicoastal relationship. Both of us got a lot more work done that way.

This conference must be full of mothers? Maybe having as hard a time as I had. I wondered what my kids felt like with a mother struggling to write all the time, so I asked them.

One daughter wrote back: "Having a Mom and Dad who were doing their art in the house made making art normal and casual and an integral part of life. It made us kids do art also."

Another daughter wrote: "Getting put to bed and hearing the sound of the typewriter and knowing your mom was right there, was reassuring." (She said, We didn't know till later Mom was putting us to bed earlier than other kids.)

My son wrote: "I remember being proud and inspired by my mother. . . . I would never have tried to write if it hadn't been for her." His note was full of how unfair it was that Ed got to do his art with no hassle and that I had to struggle for every minute. My son would fit right in here.

I want to set the record straight about me writing in a playpen. It isn't explained properly . . . and never has been, ever. OK, you put your desk in the corner of a room. You take apart one corner of a playpen and open it out. Remove the floor. Attach the corners to the walls on each side of the desk. The area will be three times again as big as a playpen. The kids are fenced out and can't reach your papers. Mostly mine were hanging over the fence talking to me. My kids did *not* yell and rage outside it, as has been written. After all, I had learned to mother from that Frenchwoman who looked after us. I wasn't quite as good as she was, but almost. The kids came first. They were happy. I was the one who wasn't. I was suffocating there. But now I have all the time to write I want.

Except when I have to write a speech.